Paula:
Live love Passion!
Valerie Clark

TORMENTED
WITHOUT A TRACE

a novel by

VALERIE CLARK

ISBN: 0-7596-7327-6

Library of Congress Control Number: 2002092190

This book is printed on acid free paper.

Printed in the United States of America
Bloomington, IN

TIGRESS ENTERTAINMENT, LLC

For information: www.tigressentertainment.com

1st Books rev. 05/16/02

To the one man who can read my every mood;
who can complete my thought a moment before I speak it;
who sends dreamlike waves of ecstasy through my body;
who knows when I need to be held and when I need to be heard.

I will always love you, Jeremy.

If I am not for myself,
who is for me?

And if not now,
when?

Hillel

BOOK I

TAINTED LOVE

Prologue

"Natalie, come on," Megan said, racing to the Alpine Cliff's ice cream shop. "Hurry up. I have so much to tell you. You are not going to believe what happened today… There I was outside my locker and Danny Mintner came right up to me and totally asked me out."

"No way," Natalie exclaimed. "You're kidding. Tell me everything."

"I'm trying," Megan said breathlessly as she opened the glass door. Small silver bells slung over the top of the door jingled, alerting the young man at the cash register that he had customers.

The girls walked up to the steel-covered counter.

"I'll have a small cup of chocolate with nuts," Megan ordered.

As Natalie began to utter her request, the young man behind the counter handed her a small cup of ice cream.

"I know," he said in a low monotone. "Banana with chocolate

sprinkles—small." He passed her the white Styrofoam cup. His brown eyes were vacant and cold, frightening Natalie.

She was bewildered briefly that he knew what she wanted. She pulled her wallet from her school bag and placed three dollars on the cold countertop without looking up at the young man.

"It's on me," he said.

Natalie didn't hear him. She had turned, leaving the money behind. Natalie was concentrating on selecting the best table so she and Megan could go into all the little details surrounding Megan's news.

The young man watched Natalie walk away. Her long chestnut curls flowed down her back, bouncing slightly with each step. She was naturally beautiful. Slim. And always smiling. She and Megan wore matching soft pink, spring parochial school uniforms.

The girls leaped into the corner booth.

"That guy's cute but he creeps me out," Megan said, referring to the young man behind the counter.

"He is cute—in an unrefined kinda way," Natalie said, distracted by a hollow glance.

In hushed conversation, Megan told Natalie that the school hunk had asked her out for Saturday night. They savored their ice cream and every word about Megan and Danny's exchange. The young man behind the counter tried to hear what they were saying, catching an occasional sentence or two.

"Oh, my God," Natalie said. "Look at the time. I have got to get home. I have a trig test tomorrow and I really have no idea. If I don't get an 'A' my father'll remind me, for a change, how stupid I am—being a girl and all. Maybe my 'Prince Charming' will sweep me off my feet too someday..."

The young man behind the counter noticed that Natalie was leaving. "I'm heading out," he shouted to the manager who was in the back of the store in the stock room. He took off his white hat and cotton apron, following Natalie on her walk home.

She noticed footsteps in back of her. Natalie glanced over her shoulder but saw no one. The young man had ducked behind a tree. She started walking faster. The footsteps behind her sped up. She began running and he began running after her. Natalie dropped her knapsack, her books and papers falling out. The stranger caught up to her and grabbed her first by the arm, then by her torso, pulling her hastily into the wooded area on the opposite side of the street. She tried to break free but he just held her tighter.

Natalie started to scream. "Sto…"

With one hand, he clutched her neck and covered her mouth with the other hand as he pushed her into the woods. Then he pulled out a knife and released the blade. Its loud metallic snap filled Natalie with terror.

Suddenly, she felt a sharp point on the side of her throat. He slit her skin and crimson blood dribbled onto her pinafore.

"You make a sound, Princess, and I'll slice you from ear to ear. It'll ruin your pretty, snot-ass outfit, you bitch."

She was gasping for air with her hands on his forearm trying to loosen his grip on her throat. He let up slightly and she jabbed him as hard as she could with her elbow in his gut. He was knocked back slightly. She broke free hoping to flee. He grabbed Natalie by her hair, turned her around, and smacked her in the face so hard she grunted in pain. She fell to the ground.

"We can do this the easy way, Princess, or the hard way."

She tried to stand up to make a run for it. He grabbed her foot and she fell face first into the ground hitting her chin on a rock. He yanked her back by her ankles toward him, dragging her on her stomach. He pushed her onto her back and straddled her. Natalie began shaking. He slit open her uniform with a red-handled switchblade exposing her bra and under-wear. He started to unbuckle his belt.

"I see you every fucking day and you don't even know who I am. Do you, Princess?"

Natalie quivered, looking up at him, staring into his angry eyes.

"You and your stuck up friends wouldn't dream of giving someone like me the time of day. I'm not a member of the 'lucky sperm club.' Sorry,

Angel. My daddy didn't have a trust fund with my name on it. He was a drunk who beat me and my mother and then took off. I bust my ass at two part-time jobs just to survive, putting myself through school doing menial shit for cunts like you. But I thought you were different at first. I guess I was wrong. One day, Princess, I'll be one of you rich folks and you'll be sorry, very sorry, you didn't notice me. But for now, Angel, you leave me no other choice." His brown eyes burned with a cold fire that seared her soul. "In order to be with you, Angel, it has to be this way this time." He leaned down and kissed her neck seductively. "That wasn't so bad. Was it, Princess?"

She drew her leg up and kneed him in the groin. He reached for a fallen tree branch that lay next to them and rammed her in the head. Blood poured from an open gash over her eyebrow. He began raping her, forcing himself into her, as she lay there helpless, terrified, tears streaming down her face. One strong thrust broke through her hymen. With each stroke, he penetrated her more deeply. She winced in pain with every pelvic gyration. He took his time, reveling in his theft of her virginity. Then it was over.

"Was it everything you thought it would be, Princess?" he asked, pulling himself slowly out of her.

Natalie spit at his face and struggled to get out from under him. She couldn't pry herself away. The weight of his body was too much for her to move.

"I just wanted to have you all to myself, Angel. Now, no one else can know you the way I do."

"Fuck you," she said with a venomous hatred.

He picked up the tree branch again and smashed her head. She laid there, unconscious, blood leaking from her scull. He pulled up his pants and buckled his belt.

"What a shame, Princess. I really did love you," he said, kneeling down. He cupped her face tenderly and kissed her now blood-soaked lips. "Rest in peace, Angel." He stood up and walked away, leaving her for dead.

Natalie woke up two days later at Kensington Hospital in Westchester, disoriented and scared with her mother by her side holding her hand. Natalie's head was wrapped with white bandages that covered one eye.

Harv, her father was in the corner of the room watching the stock market report on the mid-day news.

Adrian, her sister, sat on the other side of her in a chair.

Natalie's exposed eye fluttered from the light.

"Oh, my God, Natalie. You're awake." Her mother's eyes welled. "Adrian, go tell the nurse to get the doctor."

She ran to the nurse's station.

A doctor whisked into the room wearing traditional hospital 'blues.' "Natalie, I'm Dr. Nadler," he said. He took a small flashlight from his chest pocket and scanned the eye that was showing. "Can you hear me?"

She shook her head slightly indicating yes.

"You're in the hospital. Do you know how you got here?" he asked.

She shook her head no and started to cry.

The doctor glanced up at her mother. "It's okay, Natalie," Dr. Nadler said. "You have a concussion and some exterior wounds but you're going to be fine. Your vitals are all good and strong. We've been monitoring your brain activity and there seems to be no serious damage. It'll take you some time to get your strength back but you're going to be all right."

Dr. Nadler spoke with Natalie's parents outside her room. "We did a rape kit on your daughter and were able to get some skin and blood samples from under her nails and semen in her vagina. A detective has been calling to find out if she regained consciousness. It would be a good idea for Natalie to speak with the police. They want to get this guy."

Betsy was on the verge of tears listening to the doctor talk about her daughter. Images of the ordeal flooded her thoughts.

"Thanks for your concern," Harv said, with an impatient, angry tone. "We'll keep it in mind."

They returned to Natalie. Her mother, sobbing, patted Natalie's head. She was grateful her youngest daughter was back. "Honey, the police want to talk to you."

"Betsy, for Christ's sake!" her father exclaimed.

"Harvey, please… Do you remember anything?"

"No," Natalie said in a weak, scraggly voice.

"Do you know what this kind of publicity would do to my practice?" her father asked angrily. "She said she doesn't remember. Just leave well enough alone, Betsy, and let her get on with her life."

"I want the bastard who did this to my daughter to suffer the way he made her suffer," her mother said. "You're only thinking of yourself, for a change. This is your daughter," Betsy shouted.

Natalie knew by this exchange between her parents that she had been raped. She turned her head trying to bury her face in the pillow and began to cry.

Chapter One

It was another hectic day for Natalie on the trading floor. The market had been experiencing some turbulence in recent weeks and it was taking its toll. Her latest initial public offerings were bouncing around like roller coasters.

Around 10 AM on Tuesday while Natalie was in the middle of several deals, her secretary called out to her. "Yo, Nat, David's on your top line," she shouted above the frenzy in a thick Brooklyn accent. "He says he has to speak with you. It's important."

Concerned and distracted by the thought of abandoning the negotiation she was involved with, she asked one of her colleagues to pinch hit for her. "Nashy, I need you to reel in this baby for me. Gunta wants to sell a ten million share block of EBS. Remember in marks not yen. I'll make it up to you. Thanks."

Natalie walked into her glass-enclosed office adjacent to the trading floor, sat at her desk and picked up her phone.

"Hi," the deep voice on the other end said. "I know Sue said it was really busy there for you today, but this is far more important than whatever you were in the middle of... You know the case I've been working on? We thought it was going to go to the jury this afternoon, but we just settled. Huge."

"I'm sure my dad is dancing up and down Park Avenue," Natalie said.

"Only a little. We haven't gotten the check yet. But I want to go out tonight to celebrate. What time do you think you can get out?"

"I've got to sit down with Peter after the market closes and talk about a business trip he wants me to go on later this week. I'm not sure what it's for at the moment. He always has me take care of his offshore clients so his wife doesn't divorce him. But I should hopefully be able to get out by seven tonight."

"Pretty soon we'll get you knocked up and you won't have to deal with these ridiculous jaunts of his," David said.

"Always the poet and so supportive of my career. Thanks."

"I'll meet you in your lobby at seven. Don't be late."

She wondered if he had even heard her comment.

"Love you," he said mindlessly, like an involuntary bodily function.

"See you later," she replied without reciprocating his 'I love you.' She hung up the phone and gazed across the trading floor. Natalie was attracted to the investment-banking world by its excitement, glamour, and mystique. Working in the heart of it for the last ten years since graduate school had not changed her perspective. She didn't mind the long hours coupled with market and emotional volatility, though they left their marks, because her success was something she achieved for herself. She maintained her youthful beauty. Her long wavy chestnut locks still cascaded down her back. Natalie never believed she had to look or act like a man to get ahead. She opened the bottom drawer of her desk and reached for her purse, taking out her make up case. She pulled out a new pack of antacids, threw a handful in the back of her mouth, took a deep breath, and returned to the thriving jungle outside her office.

Peter, Natalie's boss, poked his head into her office just after the closing bell of the market sounded on CNN from the tv monitors overhead. "Hey, Nat, have a minute? I gotta cut outta here at five," he said.

"For you? Sure," she said.

Peter walked into his office. Natalie followed.

"As I mentioned this morning, I was planning on going on this trip Thursday over to Europe, but I can't take the time," he said. "Too many things are going on for me to be out. And, my wife'll have my balls for lunch if I go. I'm supposed to meet with Papa Santiago and the 'heir-apparent' in Cannes. Have dinner with them. Find out about their succession plans. Learn more about the division they want to sell off. Then be their guest at this bash. There's some black tie Friday night celebrating a billion years in business... You know he's my biggest client. Can't let him down. So I have to send you. You can talk business and charm the pants off of these guys at the same time. Show 'em your 'T and A' and they'll love me for it."

Natalie glared at him.

"Talents and abilities," he said. "A little cleavage and thigh wouldn't hurt."

"And what else?" Natalie said.

"That's it."

"That's never just it with you, Pete. Your trips usually include sixteen-hour days and back-to-back client meetings. I'm not convinced. Are you whoring me out again?" Her teeth clenched and her nostrils flared. "You know I'm getting married next month."

"That's all there is to it. In fact, take a few days on me. You've been busting that cute little ass of yours a lot lately for me. Just to show you I'm not shitting you. Okay?"

"If I have to sit cooped up in a plane for six to eight hours each way just for a frickin' dinner plus get all 'perttied up,' and deal with the God damn time change... how you even have the nerve to ask me when my wedding is right around the corner and you know I'm going crazy over all the nasty little annoying last minute details... I'm taking the week, Pete."

"I love when you get all fiery on me. It turns me on. Wish my wife did. Just get someone to stoke all those irons you have in the fire while you're gone, no problem. Anyway, just let me know. Oh, by the way, here's the S.E. file so you can get up to speed." Peter shoved a manila folder in Natalie's hand that had 'Santiago Enterprises' written on it.

She left his office on the prowl to find some unsuspecting workaholic to take care of her clients while she's out of the office. "Hey Nashy, how did you do with Gunta earlier?" she asked. "Were you able to find enough fools to buy that block of dogs he was selling?"

"Not a problem, Nat."

"You're the best… Hey, would you be able to take over for me for a week? Pete wants me to do him a favor. Now I need one. We're all just one big happy family here. I would really appreciate it and I promise I won't ask you to cover for me while I'm on my honeymoon."

"Where's Pete sending you?"

"South of France."

"Poor baby. How will you ever survive? Just bring me back some nice red wine you Americans think tastes good and we'll call it even."

"You got it. You're the best."

"Sue, I need you to make some travel arrangements," she said to her secretary. "Book me out of JFK to Paris for tomorrow for one night. Then on to Nice Friday morning with a hotel in Cannes Friday through Wednesday returning Thursday out of Nice and messenger the tickets to my apartment tonight."

"Do you need a car anywhere?"

"Just to the airport tomorrow. Thanks."

A few minutes after seven, Natalie grabbed her bag and dashed off to meet David downstairs.

He stood at the corner of the elevator bank looking at his Cartier wristwatch, scowling, as she rushed off the elevator. "Seven o'clock means when the big hand is on the twelve and the little hand is on the seven," David said in a condescending tone. "It always amazes me they pay you the money they do when you can't even tell time. We have reservations at Bella. You knew this was a special evening for me."

Natalie was indifferent to his criticism, glad to have escaped two hours earlier than usual.

He kissed her cheek and put his arm around the small of her back to hasten her step toward a taxi.

When they arrived at the dimly lit Italian restaurant on the upper west side, Natalie was still disturbed from their telephone conversation earlier in the day. She needed assistance in order to feel relaxed and not argumentative with David.

"Right this way, Mr. Hughes," the maitre d' said, escorting them to their table. "May I get you something from the bar?"

"How about a bottle of '98 Chateau Calais Merlot?" Natalie suggested.

"The lady certainly has fine taste," the maitre d' said leaving them to their privacy seated at the candlelit table.

"My mother called today and asked how we were doing with the plans for the wedding," David said. "We're only six weeks away and she said the invitations should have gone out by now. How are you coming with them?" he asked sternly.

Natalie looked into his eyes but there was no emotional connection.

He did not gaze lovingly at her. David could never see into her soul.

She didn't respond to his question. Natalie turned her head to look out the window and watch the lonely walkers on Columbus Avenue rushing by. "I don't want to talk about this right now..." she said, her voice distant.

David frowned.

"...They're at the engraver's along with the list. He said they'd be in the mail tomorrow. Okay? Can we talk about wedding plans another time?"

"Now you're sure all the firm's partners are on the guest list?"

"That would still technically be wedding plans," she interrupted.

"Right... Well, we're here to celebrate my closing this deal. Like I was saying on the phone, Jackman was afraid the jury was going to find for Unitor, the developer, my client, so he convinced his client to settle."

"This is the one where the builder knowingly put in that substandard wiring and all those people were hurt in a fire? How can you be happy making money off of this?"

Her questions did not register. David continued as if she had not spoken. "I was brilliant. My closing remarks were award winning. You should have seen me. I turned this loser of a case into big bucks for the firm." David could only converse about himself. He never expressed any interest in asking Natalie how her day had gone. At best, he would speak to her in response to something she would utter, but he never really heard her. Why would this night be any different?

"I'll be leaving tomorrow for a week," Natalie jutted in.

David stared at her blankly.

She shared with him the details, as she knew them surrounding the business trip to Europe. "I'm going to take some time for myself while I'm there. I know it's a crazy time to be gone, but Adrian's on top of everything like it's her wedding instead of mine."

"That's fine," he said.

Her heart sank. Although she desperately needed the time off, she would have done anything to hear him say for her not to stay away so long because he would miss her. Or even that he would join her. Natalie was perpetually hurt because David never needed her. She had hoped to hear something over the last two years of their courtship that would lead her to believe that he was 'the one'—her soul mate. But there had been nothing. Natalie felt they were simply on autopilot.

For the remainder of the evening, David continued to impress himself by talking ceaselessly about his work. He was oblivious that Natalie was tuning him out. He lacked the ability to read an individual and always assumed Natalie's mood mirrored his.

She didn't love him. It was only the security a relationship could provide that she loved—someone to take care of her emotional needs. But that was not David. Natalie thought herself spoiled. How could she not love this man? He was handsome, very well off financially. He had been wooed by the top law firms in the country when he graduated from Harvard Law. Deep inside, these things didn't matter to her though. She needed to be held, told she was beautiful. The injured little girl that dwelled within her was afraid to be alone. Though she embodied strength as a successful career woman, Natalie craved to be loved, nurtured.

David was everything a woman should want, Natalie's father told her, and she should think herself lucky that any man could love her the way her innocence was soiled. He insisted that Natalie accept David's marriage proposal a year ago when she wanted to say no and hold out for her soul mate.

"Are you staying with me tonight?" Natalie asked when the waiter brought the check.

"Love to, but can't. I can come up just for a little while. Have an early morning meeting on a new case and I haven't read the file yet."

She wanted to be close to him especially since it would be a while before they could see each other again. She craved some reassurance of his love. It wasn't going to happen this night or any other. She knew what he meant by 'a little while.' He would pleasure himself in her and then be gone.

They walked along Central Park West to her apartment building.

"Good evening, Ms. Baylor," the doorman said, handing her an envelope from Air France.

"Thanks, John," she said, walking toward the elevator. David followed.

Natalie kicked off her shoes once inside the apartment and walked across her ornate Persian rug. She opened the envelope, ensuring her itinerary was what she specified to Sue late that afternoon.

David reached around her unzipping Natalie's skirt and pulled her underwear down. He kissed her. There was no spark, no passion, no sharing of innermost thoughts. His cursory touch turned her off. Sex felt as though it were scripted. Hollow. Once a week he initiated a sexual encounter. There was no creativity, just a mechanical sequence. She could predict each move before it was executed and the amount of time it would take. When she wore something sexy like lingerie, he would not notice. If she began any physical initiative—kissing, cuddling, or massage, he would always have something else he needed to get to within a minute or two, like a brief for a case he was working on, or phone calls needing to be returned to clients, work comrades, or his men's club drinking buddies.

He dropped his pants to his ankles and bent Natalie forward. He pushed himself into her to satisfy only his needs. At the peak of arousal, David pulled out, ejaculating on her buttocks. It was a power trip, not making love. When he finished, he wiped himself and a little bit of blood from the last day of her period on her cast off panties and pulled up his pants.

"Call me when you get back," David said. He kissed Natalie on her cheek and then went downstairs to hail a cab to get himself home to the upper east side.

She did not believe he would be thinking of her. Natalie felt he would only be thinking of his work and the pursuit of money.

After cleaning herself up, Natalie strapped on her telephone headset to leave a voice mail for Peter. "Hey, Pete. Natalie. Sue got my travel plans set for tomorrow. I'm going a day early so I'm not too jet lagged when I meet Santiago and son. I'll be back in the office next Thursday. Nashiro is going to cover my book. We'll call it even. Ciao."

She walked over to her jewelry box, taking off her engagement ring. When she opened the drawer, the tiny dancer music box began to chime, 'It's a Small World After All.' A gift from her mother when she was seven. Natalie watched the little ballerina twirl while the music played. Suddenly, her mind was flooded with the memory of walking into the ice cream shop on the day she was raped. The tinkling chimes reminded her of the bells jingling over the door. She quickly slammed the small drawer shut.

To distract her thoughts she grabbed the remote and channel surfed to find a re-run of Seinfeld. Natalie put on her Victoria Secret's nightshirt and reached for Chuckles, her favorite teddy bear. He gave her comfort when she was afraid or lonely. She had dozens of stuffed bears from around the world that kept him company in all sizes, shapes, and colors carefully placed throughout her apartment. Her home was decorated like an antique doll house. Natalie tucked herself and her stuffed friend into bed. She held him close until she drifted off to sleep with the drone of the television in the background.

Chapter Two

The alarm startled Natalie out of a sound sleep at 7 AM. It felt good to her sleeping in for a change. The television was still playing. She shambled into the kitchen half asleep and pulled a banana off of a freckled bunch sitting on the edge of the counter. She plopped some yogurt, ice cubes, and the peeled banana into the blender, whipping up her pre-workout drink. The sun was glistening on the reservoir beyond her window. Natalie downed her fruit beverage, put on her spandex running shorts with a matching top, and put her hair in a ponytail pulling it through the back of her Winnie the Pooh baseball cap. She slipped into her sneakers then grabbed her sunglasses from the wooden vestibule table as she pulled the front door shut behind her. Natalie went for a three-mile jog in the park. It had been at least a year since she had a day off during the week. It seemed as though everyone around her was racing to work. This felt like a total luxury.

When she arrived back at her apartment, she showered. While she was packing, Natalie telephoned her mother with her phone headset on. "Hey, Ma. It's me."

"How are you, dear?" her mother asked with concern. I get nervous when I don't hear from you every day. Is everything all right?"

"Yesterday was just very busy. Pete's got me going over to France to meet one of his clients so I'm going to stay over a few extra days. I wanted to let you know I'm heading out in a few minutes. Sue has my itinerary if you need me."

"How is everything between you and David? Remember, dear, it gets a little rocky just before the big day. You are going to be so beautiful."

"We're the same as usual."

"He's a good man, Natalie. He'll take care of you. Don't say anything but... after he settled this big case yesterday, your father said he's going to make him partner before the end of the year. You won't have to work. You can make babies like Adrian."

"Ma, I don't want to be like Adrian. She's overweight and miserable because she doesn't have a life or an identity she can call her own. If it wasn't for this wedding and my intense work schedule, she'd have nothing to do."

"Have you reconsidered taking David's name?"

"No. I'm not taking his name. Why would I? I already have one."

"It would really be better for his business if you did, dear."

"What about me and my business? My clients all know me by my last name. What about me—period? Daddy is looking at this as a great financial merger between our families. Adrian thinks this is the wedding she never had 'cause she was too stupid to use a condom. And you, Mother, of all people, you should understand."

"Do you love him, Natalie?"

Natalie was silent.

"Honey, it's okay. In time you can grow to love him."

"Yeah and it's been thirty-eight years, Mother. Do you love Daddy?"

The silence on the telephone grew long and oppressive.

"If you don't love him, no one is forcing you to get married," her mother said finally. "I suppose you should choose who and what's right for you, not what other people think is right for you. You always have, your whole life. Why would this be any different?"

"Yeah, right," Natalie snapped sarcastically.

"Your father will get over it eventually. I wish sometimes I had your inner strength. Today women don't have to make the choices we did when I was young. I'll love you no matter what you choose."

Natalie heard the intercom buzz. "Mom, I have to go. My car service is here. I'll talk to you when I get back." She took her headset off and closed her suitcase.

"Will you hold my mail for the week, Felix?" she said to the morning doorman when she got downstairs with her luggage.

"No problem, Ms. Baylor. Have a good trip," he replied, opening the door to the black sedan.

"We're taking you to JFK today?" the driver asked.

"Yes. Air France, please." She rolled down the smoked window to let the warm summer air hit her face. She thought about what her mother said on the drive out to Queens but Natalie knew she had no choice but to marry David. To face the harshness of her father's anger if she disobeyed his wishes would be worse, in her mind, than spending her life with someone she didn't love.

Natalie couldn't see herself as an adult. In her heart she was still fifteen, not realizing she did not have to sublimate her needs to her father's to avoid his emotional abuse. She could not grasp or acknowledge that her emancipation from him was a choice she could make.

Before Natalie knew it, the car stopped to drop her off at international departures. She wheeled her luggage into the terminal to check in.

As Natalie approached the ticket counter, she noticed her tickets were in business class. "Those damn bean counters," she muttered to herself. "Can you move me up to first class?" Natalie asked while handing the desk attendant her ticket.

"I'm sorry, you'll have to ask them to do that at the gate," the clerk responded. "Passport, please. Thanks. Here are your tickets. You're all set."

When Natalie got to her gate, there was a long line at check-in, so she sat down to wait. The terminal was packed. She took the only empty seat available near the counter.

The man seated in the next chair working on his laptop gave her the 'once over look' from head to toe. He was handsome, she thought. He glanced at her and smiled.

The moment their eyes locked, she felt a familiarity with him—an instant connection like she knew him from somewhere else. Natalie smiled back while she organized her travel documents.

He closed his laptop. "Are you looking to check in?" he asked in a soft voice.

"Yeah."

"It's so crowded. I thought I would wait too."

"Why is it so jammed today?" she asked. "It's like they're giving out free tickets."

"Are you traveling for business or pleasure?" His brown eyes looked at her intently.

"It's for business but I am turning it into pleasure. Some badly needed R&R. How 'bout yourself?"

"Pretty much the same but I live over there. So I'm sort of going home. I'm Jeremy, by the way," he said in a low, sensual voice leaning closer to her.

"Natalie. Nice to meet you."

"Wow! I can't help but notice that rock you're wearing. It's blinding. Someone loves you."

"Something like that."

"Okaaay," he said drawing out his response indicating that he didn't fully understand her remark.

"The line's shorter now," Natalie said, pointing at the counter.

"Yeah. I better do the same."

Natalie stepped up to the representative at the desk to try and get her seat assignment changed.

Jeremy overheard her conversation.

"Is there anyway you can bump me up to first?"

"Let me see what we can do." The attendant fiddled with a few buttons and saw that Natalie was a very frequent flyer. "That should be no problem. I have you in first class, Ms. Baylor. It's not a very full flight. We should be boarding in about ten minutes." The woman behind the counter handed Natalie her boarding pass. "Here you go. Have a good trip."

"Thanks very much. I appreciate your help."

Jeremy smiled at Natalie as she passed. She returned the smile, walking past him to her seat. His eyes dropped to admire her gym-tightened glutes.

"Can you get me next to my colleague who just checked in?" Jeremy asked the desk attendant. "I'm already booked in first."

"Yes. The seat next to her is still available."

"Great. Thanks." He returned to sit with Natalie.

"So, how long are you going to be in Paris?"

"Just for one night and then I fly to Nice, but I'll be staying in Cannes. And you?"

"I have some business to attend to in Paris but I have a home on the beach in the south that I'm headed to for a few weeks."

"Oh, that sounds great."

"Come on along."

Natalie was silent though her interest was piqued.

Jeremy felt her hesitation and quickly changed the subject. "So what do you do when you're not in airports?"

"I'm an investment banker on Wall Street."

"Beautiful *and* smart. And I would imagine very comfortable financially too. Not bad. Does this man of yours know how lucky he is?"

Natalie smiled. "And what do you do?"

"I'm an investor for the most part. I buy and sell real estate, art, business concerns. I like to acquire things. Whatever makes sense. Whatever interests me. Looks like they're boarding. Where are you sitting?"

"3A," Natalie said

"You mean I have the honor of sitting next to you all the way to the 'City of Lights.' How did I get so lucky?" When they started walking toward the jet way, Jeremy put his arm around her back. He looked Natalie up and down soaking in the view.

She caught him and laughed.

"Busted. Just admiring a beautiful work of art. It's what I do. And a work of art you are."

They walked through the ramp onto the plane and to their seats.

"Let me help you with that," Jeremy said, placing her bag in the overhead compartment. "Anything you need out of here?"

"No. I've got my book in my purse. Thanks."

They settled into their seats.

"So let me see what your reading."

She reached into her bag and handed him a paperback.

"'SUMMIT: The Achievement of Happiness and Success—The Practical and Spiritual Approach.' You're into self-improvement I see."

"24/7. I always want something more—to do better for myself, my life, in meeting my goals and being happy in the process."

"I'm right there with you." He reached into his bag under the seat in front of him and pulled out a small leather loose-leaf notebook. He unzipped it. "I've got my daily goals, weekly, monthly, quarterly, yearly. And I write what my experiences are in getting to them and making them happen every day."

"Seems like we have a lot in common," Natalie remarked.

"I can only hope."

"Since you asked me... is there anyone special in your life?" Natalie inquired.

"There was a long time ago but... it didn't work out."

"What went wrong?"

"I wasn't good enough for her."

"Was that her opinion or yours?"

Jeremy paused and went somewhere else for a moment. He didn't answer.

"Did you love her?"

"Yeah. I really loved her..." He glanced away, then gestured at her ring. "Tell me, does your very generous man know how lucky he is? You didn't answer me before."

"I didn't think you really wanted an answer to that. I thought you were just making conversation."

"And… the answer is…?"

"Honestly? I don't know the answer to that."

"Do you love him?"

Natalie was silent. Awkward.

"Okaaay. When's the big day?"

"Let's see. What's today? Six weeks from Saturday," she said looking at her watch.

"Invitations out yet?"

"Christ! What is it with the invitations?"

"Oooo. Touchy subject."

Natalie laughed at her glaring over-sensitivity. "Sorry about that." She felt instantly comfortable to be herself around him.

"It's probably not appropriate for me to ask this but does he tell you how beautiful you are?"

She looked into his eyes. "No. He doesn't," she replied with sadness.

"May I get you something to drink?" the flight attendant interrupted. They were both oblivious that the plane had taken off.

"Perrier with lime, if you have it," Natalie responded.

"And for you, sir?"

"The same. Thanks. My favorite beverage. Another thing we have in common. Not that it's any of my business… back to 'Mr. Wonderful…'

If you're not in love with him, why are you planning to marry him?"

"I looked for my 'Mr. Right' but he never came along. At this point, companionship would be nice. And besides, my father... well, never mind."

"You sound like you're ancient. Come on. You have everything going for you and you feel like you have to take what showed up?" Jeremy challenged.

"It's not that simple," Natalie asserted.

"Maybe finding 'Mr. Right' isn't easy but did you look with an open heart? We should only marry someone we love. You just told me a minute ago you go for your goals in order to find happiness. Wouldn't that be a goal?"

"Yeah, well not all goals have been met. Sometimes that's life," she said with frustration.

"Describe your perfect soul mate to me," he asked.

When Jeremy said 'soul mate,' his eyes held hers and a warmth spread through her body. Time seemed to stop for an instant. Natalie felt innately connected to him. He understood her. This concept of being someone's soul mate was incomprehensible to David. When she mentioned intimacy to him, he would always ask what she meant and never really fully absorbed the concept. He lived in a tangible, fact-based world. Natalie would try and probe his psyche, but was met with neutrality and blank stares. He had no idea what she was talking about. To David, an intimate conversation meant they talked about the weather, current events—something other than his career and the acquisition of money. Their conversations rendered her emotionally bored, starving for intimacy. Anything of any depth was foreign to David. She hungered for someone to be interested in hearing about her most private thoughts and dreams.

Natalie answered his question after a moment of reflection. "My soul mate is someone who's loving, caring, passionate about life, who knows what makes me tick and someone who wants to tick with me. I can provide all the comforts of life for myself. I don't need a man to be able to do that for me. This is not a concept my fiancé gets at all. We share similar socio-economic backgrounds, but that's it. He's about the pursuit of financial and political gain. I'm about the pursuit of love and mutual enjoyment and exploration of that love. All the men I've met have been like 'Mr. Wonderful' as you call him. Enough of me… And what's your perfect love goddess like?" Natalie asked.

"I think I'm looking at her," Jeremy replied. His eyes caressed her.

Natalie blushed slightly. She felt that Jeremy knew her intuitively.

The flight attendant returned with their drinks.

"Here's to getting to know each other better and better…" Jeremy toasted.

They clicked glasses and sipped their effervescing water. Natalie and Jeremy talked while the other passengers watched the movie or tried to sleep. Their conversation became deeper and more personal. They barely touched the meals that were set in front of them. When they spoke, their lips were no more than a few inches from one another.

"Tell me, I bet you were one of those super popular prom queens with tons of guys vying for your attention," Jeremy remarked.

"Not really," Natalie responded. "I was pretty shy in school. I kind of withdrew at the point all of my friends started to date."

"Why is that?"

Natalie looked down for a moment. She felt safe enough to share with him something she was never comfortable enough to tell David. "I was raped when I was fifteen. I've always been cautious since then."

"I'm so sorry... I'm sure it was a horrible experience. Was it some-one you knew?"

"Maybe," Natalie answered. "I was knocked unconscious and didn't regain a full memory of it. My parents have been very protective of me as a result."

Jeremy stroked her cheek. "If you were mine, I would do every-thing I could to keep you safe and protect you from being hurt."

From the window of the plane, they watched the shimmering hues of the sun begin to emerge around six o'clock in their new time zone. To Natalie, the spectrum of colors appeared more vibrant with Jeremy by her side. As she occupied the seat closest to the window, Jeremy leaned into her to see the teal, blood orange, and magenta sky unfold. When the captain dropped the flight gear to prepare for landing at *Charles de Gaulle* nausea swept over Natalie like a gray cloud at the thought of this encounter coming to an end.

"Are you okay?" Jeremy asked. He noticed a look of breathlessness in Natalie. He took her hand and then caressed her face.

She did not want the plane to land. Natalie wanted to stay suspended in time captive to Jeremy's attention. She knew she had met her soul mate and in minutes he would be gone forever.

They walked to the baggage claim area together in silence mourning the end of their exchange. Natalie reached for her luggage when it spun around on the carousel. Jeremy pulled it off the conveyer setting it down beside them. Together they stood staring into each other's eyes in the midst of the throng of travelers whirring around them though they felt as if they were the only ones for miles. They edged closer to one another both wanting to kiss. They lingered a moment and then embraced in a penetrating hug. Natalie's soft cheek pressed against his face. His warm skin comforted her. Closing her eyes, she inhaled the scent of his cologne as if it were her last breath of oxygen piercing the sensory memory of it in her mind. They held onto one another, each not wanting to release the other. Jeremy ran his hands up and down her slender back. She ran her fingers through his light brown hair.

"I don't want to let you go. If I do, you'll be gone forever," he said.

After feeling like time had stopped for a few moments, they both loosened their embrace and pulled slightly away. Jeremy held her hand and then raised it to his lips kissing it, smelling the sweet perfume on her wrist. They walked to the taxi stand outside slowly as if they were headed down a dark, sinister alley. The finality of their encounter was sinking in. Cloaked in his arms was the only place Natalie wanted to be.

"Please tell me I'm going to see you again," Jeremy said.

She was silent, torn between her commitment to David and the life-long yearning that now had a name and a face.

Jeremy handed the taxi dispatcher Natalie's bag. A cab pulled up. The driver got out and walked around opening the door for her.

She kissed Jeremy's cheek. He had his answer.

"A quel hôtel, Mademoiselle?"

She did not hear.

"Where to, miss?"

Finally she answered. *"La rive droit—L'Hôtel de Lyon, s'il vous plaît,"* Natalie said to the driver mindlessly. Getting into the car, she was transfixed by Jeremy's face as he watched her leave. She felt a piece of her was fading slowly away as her taxi drove off. Natalie didn't know if she did the right thing by not agreeing to see Jeremy again. She wanted to be faithful to David even though she didn't love him. But the possibility of being with someone she was truly connected to weakened her ability to see things clearly. She was starving for love and meaningful affection. Her father had sheltered her after the rape by not allowing her to date until she left home. She had become fearful of any close connection to a male. But Natalie somehow felt safe with Jeremy as if he already knew her intimately.

The taxi dropped Natalie in front of her hotel on *rue Caumartin*, a narrow street near the opera. The concierge carried her bag to the desk inside.

"Bonjour, Mademoiselle..." He rattled on in French. Though she was fluent, Natalie did not hear a word. She saw his lips moving but nothing penetrated her other senses. Missing Jeremy, she walked zombie-like to the little elevator in the corner with her bag slung over her shoulder and her key in her hand. Once in her room, Natalie opened the shutters to a charming courtyard. She began to unpack, hanging up her clothes and laying out all her fragrant toiletries on the bed. The telephone rang, startling her slightly.

"Hi. It's me," the deep, sexy voice said.

She smiled and her stomach got jittery.

"It was a mistake to let you slip away," Jeremy said. "I am so thankful I heard you tell the driver where you were staying."

She closed her eyes, mesmerized by the sound of his soft voice.

"I have to see you again," he continued. "I can't let you go. You're only here for one night. Would you please, please spend it with me? I can't stop thinking of you, the smell of your perfume, …your eyes, …your tiny waist. I'm missing you like crazy. God. I have to see you again. Natalie, will you have dinner with me tonight? I'm begging…"

"We'll save the begging for later," she said to cut the tension and nervous excitement stirring within her.

He laughed.

Natalie couldn't remember ever feeling this way. "I can't stop thinking about you either."

"Oh, my God. Tell me I'm not dreaming. I can't wait to see you. How 'bout I pick you up at seven at your hotel?"

"Sounds perfect. I'll see you then."

When she hung up the phone she was smiling so hard she held her cheeks with her hands. Natalie looked in the beveled mirror above the bureau in her room and began talking to her reflection. "I'm actually going to spend time with someone who wants to be with me. Not with my inheritance after my father dies. What a great feeling. So this is what happiness is like. Wow... What am I gonna to wear? In Paris. Have credit cards. I'm going shopping."

She washed her face and put on a little floral sun dress and sandals. She gave herself five hours to find the perfect dress. Natalie walked up and down *rue du Faubourg St. Honoré* and *Avenue Montaigne* with the sun gleaming down on her while peering into the windows and browsing through *Chanel, Yves St. Laurent,* and all the stylish *haute couture* boutiques. She was served sparkling water, champagne, and exotic coffees. Natalie tried on dozens of outfits not looking for a moment at the price tags where there was one or inquiring as to the cost where there wasn't. She didn't care. Natalie wanted to look and feel beautiful for one night. At a tiny shop, she saw a dress that looked just right hanging in the window.

"This is the last one, *Mademoiselle*," the sales girl said in a thick French accent and offered to take it out of the window. Natalie tried it on and it fit like it was made for her.

On the way back to the hotel, Natalie bought some fresh fruit, bread and cheese for her to eat while she got ready. She showered and then telephoned the concierge to see if she could get her hair, nails, and make-up done in the beauty salon downstairs. He told her to come down whenever she was ready. Natalie's excitement overcame her weariness from the flight and time change. She could not wait to see Jeremy again, to look into his eyes, to feel his warm skin against hers.

Chapter Three

At precisely seven, the phone rang in her room. Jeremy called on his cell phone from outside the hotel lobby.

"Hey, beautiful. Do you know I met the most amazing woman and she agreed to have dinner with me tonight?"

"You'll have to tell me all about it," she replied.

"I'm outside the lobby whenever you're ready."

"I'll be right down," Natalie said.

She looked at her engagement ring on her left hand and thought for a minute. She took it off and put it in her purse.

When she exited the elevator Jeremy was just turning around. He stood gazing at her through the double glass doors that were held open by golden rope swagged to the side. He nearly stumbled when he spotted her.

"Wow," he mouthed to her as she edged toward him.

He wore a black Italian double-breasted suit with a black priest-collared shirt. The sleeves were pushed up revealing his tanned forearms. His polished silver belt buckle glimmered. Her white chiffon skirt blew whimsically when she entered the lobby from the draft of the fans overhead. A halter-top pushed her breasts up where they were just peeking over the top of the v-shaped fabric.

"Hi," she said with a playful grin.

He stood silently gleaming, gazing into her eyes. She felt warm inside. No one had ever looked at her that way before. She noticed that he became aroused and loved that he responded to her physically. She had gone to great lengths to evoke this type of reaction in David when they would attend special celebrations together, but always to no avail. This was the first time in her life she felt that someone really did think she was beautiful.

"There's an art gallery with a roof top garden overlooking the Seine near the *pont du Carrousel* where I thought we could have a drink before dinner. I made reservations at a special restaurant off of the *Champs Elysees*. Will you be able to walk a little bit with those shoes?"

"Paris is a walking city like New York. I'm ready. These shoes aren't too bad."

"Smart girl. She thinks ahead. Like it." He took her arm and placed it in his cupping her hand around his bicep. "Ah... Life is good,

Lord. By the way, if you didn't already pick up on it when I was drooling outside your hotel, you look amazing."

"Oh, this old thing?" she said, referring to her new dress. "…just a little frock I tossed on moments before you arrived."

He laughed.

"Actually, I bought it just for you—for tonight."

"I thought you were going to say you made it and then I really would have thought I was dreaming. You would be the totally perfect woman. But if you bought it here, it must have cost you a fortune. Thank you. That was very thoughtful."

"I wanted to wear something special for you."

"Trust me. You've already gotten your money's worth out of it."

They strolled along the tree-lined street next to the river while the water and sun rippled in concert. Cars whirred past them as they chatted. Natalie was still holding the upper portion of his arm giving a light intermittent squeeze. They stopped to look across the river. A dozen or more birds were swooping down and rising up in an aerial game.

"Can I ask how you and your fiancé met?"

"My father introduced us. David is one of his 'golden boys' at his law firm and thought he would be ideal for me."

"What made him think that?"

"Ivy league grad… comes from money… makes lots of money…

wears ridiculously expensive suits... That stuff impresses my father. At the time I wasn't dating anyone else. It was comfortable. Safe."

"So you're doing this to please daddy?" He turned to face her. "What about pleasing Natalie?" he asked, delicately moving the hair that fell against her cheek.

She dropped her head and eyes staring down at the cobbled stones. Natalie could not look at him to answer that question.

Jeremy lifted her chin with his right index finger and kissed her soft lips. She was taken off guard. She felt as though she had craved the touch of his lips for a lifetime. She seemed to lose consciousness, eyes closed, his lips pressed delicately against hers. She was in an ethereal trance.

"Natalie, I could fall in love with you."

His words bathed her in an emotional waterfall of affection, penetrating her private self. The gentle wind blew the wisps of her hair across her glowing face as she looked up at him. Natalie wanted to tell him that she was falling in love with him. She stood mesmerized peering into the depth of his soulful eyes. Like Narcissus stood gazing at the beauty of his own reflection, Natalie felt beautiful losing herself in Jeremy's internal portrait of her. Was he a sycophant only looking to seduce her? She prayed he was genuine. Natalie wanted to be loved, needed to feel nurtured.

"I lose all track of time with you. Who would have thought a flight from New York to Paris would feel like five minutes? And now we've walked by the gallery with the garden a while ago. I wasn't even thinking about it. It's getting late. I guess we better head on to the restaurant. Why don't we get a taxi, if that's all right with you."

"I'm beginning to feel that I would want to go anywhere with you," she said. Natalie thought if she could fit in his coat pocket the rest of her life—sheltered from the outside world—that would be ideal.

There was a taxi rank across the street with two cabs waiting.

"La Tasse d'Or, s'il vous plaît," Jeremy said to the driver.

"Pas du problème," the driver replied.

Jeremy put his arm around Natalie while they drove toward their destination. She snuggled back into him—her body melting into his. She felt completely safe.

The driver stopped in front of an unmarked burgundy canopy. A gentleman dressed in a tuxedo rushed to open the door to the taxi. They were escorted through the restaurant to a small private garden in the back that was outlined with lush trees and fragrant flowers. The garden was aglow with candles. Vintage wrought-iron tables and chairs were dressed with crisp white linen tablecloths and floral cushions. A small fountain was the centerpiece of the courtyard. In the background, the trickling of water and the music of Pavarotti further engulfed their spirits. The sommelier brought a silver standing champagne bucket placing it next to their table. It was chilling a bottle of *Cristal*.

"*Monsieur*," the sommelier said, presenting the bottle to Jeremy.

Jeremy nodded in approval.

The sommelier poured a small taste in Jeremy's glass.

He swirled it around in his mouth. "*Parfait.*"

"That bottle probably cost what I spent on this dress," Natalie said.

"And *I* wanted to do something special just for you – for tonight," Jeremy replied. "There will be no menus to be bothered with. I didn't want to waste a precious second of our time together so I took care of ordering this afternoon and asked them to prepare an amazing meal for us."

"A man who thinks ahead. Like it," she said. "Did you get all your business taken care of this afternoon?"

"Yes. I did. I had to rearrange some funds for an investment opportunity I'm considering. But who wants to talk about business. All I want to do is throw this table over to the side and kiss you for an hour. That kiss by the river was amazing. It was the most perfect kiss ever. And if we kiss like that, oh my God, I can only imagine what it would be like when we…"

"When we… what?" she asked playfully.

"When we make love... When you allow me to totally ravage your body."

"You say 'when' like it will definitely happen."

"I guess that was hopeful of me. And lest we forget you're marrying someone who you don't love... to maybe gain the positive favor of your father. Ah yes, that's a far better choice than spending the rest of your life with your soul mate who will worship and adore you for eternity."

The truth of his words was sobering to Natalie. She looked away.

"Tell me, am I in this alone?" Jeremy asked. "Tell me you don't feel it too." He took both of her hands in his. "Look at me and tell me you are not falling in love with me, Natalie."

She turned back to face him. "I started falling for you about half way over the Atlantic but..."

"But what?" he asked.

"Can we just enjoy tonight?" she asked.

And they did. Sipping champagne, they fed each other fondue on long thin forks that became erotically inspiring toys turning their dining experience into a sexually charged art form. Natalie speared a morsel of bread then twirled it in the piping-hot, aromatic cheese. She offered it to Jeremy. While the gooey cheese dripped slowly into the crock, Jeremy swooped under it, licking it off the bread. He returned the favor. He seductively blew on the bite he prepared for Natalie. Cooling it to taste. He teased and taunted her, offering it to her and then pulling it back.

"Do you really want it?" he asked.

"Yes," she said.

"If you really want it, you'll have to take it."

She reached for his hand and pulled off the cheese-soaked bread with her teeth, biting the excess cheese from the fork.

They reveled in a dessert of chocolate soufflé. Jeremy submerged a strawberry into the chocolate-and-raspberry sauce drizzled over the soufflé and placed it between his lips. Leaning forward, Natalie's lips met his as they bit into the tasty morsel together, finishing their nibble kissing. They savored every bite of their private bacchanal. After the last bit of chocolate was lapped up, he took her hand and pulled her up from her chair.

Jeremy looked at his watch. "Come on," he said.

They left the restaurant and walked swiftly to the *Etoile,* dodging cars from every direction speeding to the *Arc de Triomphe.* At midnight they kissed under the arch. They taxied to the Eiffel Tower. It was all-aglow. They sat on the marble plaza at *Trocadero,* soaking in the beauty surrounding them.

"It's no wonder Paris is called the 'City of Lights,'" Natalie said.

They walked with their hands clenched tightly together in a symbiotic grasp, trying somehow to hold onto each other for eternity. Jeremy took Natalie back to her hotel around 3 AM. Just outside *l'Hôtel de Lyon,* he stopped to gaze at Natalie. Basking in his attention, she felt whole, healed from the hollow pain that dwelled within since the loss of the innocence of her youth.

" I would like to come in and… but only if you want me to," Jeremy said.

She could not answer him.

"I want to be close to you. We can just sleep holding each other."

Natalie was silent, looking off in the distance.

"I have to see you again, Natalie. This can't be it."

She feared the words she was about to utter.

"Are you thinking about your man back home?"

"Yes, I am," she said apologetically.

"I understand. I don't like it but... I don't want you to do anything that you would feel badly about... Can we please stay in touch? I can't let the most wonderful woman I have ever met just slip through my fingers. Is there any way I can talk to you or see you again? Maybe 'Mr. Wonderful' will really screw up and it'll be my lucky day."

"Here's my cell phone number," Natalie said. She wrote it down on the matches she had taken from the restaurant and handed it to him.

Jeremy reached in his jacket pocket. "This card has all of my numbers here and in the States," he said, tucking it into her purse. He grabbed Natalie and held her tight not wanting to let her go.

For a lifetime, she had longed for this. It was surreal to her, especially knowing that it would be only a memory, gone, in seconds. She felt far more nurtured and safe in Jeremy's arms than with her teddy bear, Chuckles, who had been her only source of physical comfort her entire life. She wished Chuckles had been replaced.

Jeremy kissed her long and passionately under the street lamp outside her hotel.

Natalie wanted desperately to invite him in. She hungered to feel his skin next to hers—to lay naked with him and surrender herself completely in body and spirit. Her thoughts were swimming, dazed from yearning for him her whole life. Natalie turned and walked away leaving Jeremy standing there alone watching her leave him—again. As she felt his piercing stare on her back, she knew she was in love with him—a type of love she would never have for David—for anyone.

Chapter Four

In her hotel room, Natalie lay restless in her bed thinking about Jeremy. Over and over, she compared him to David in her mind. How could she feel so strongly for someone she had just met and so little for a man whom she knew so well? The first glimmer of light crept through the sheer chiffon-like curtains around 6 AM. After not sleeping for a moment, Natalie felt hung over. She had a 10 AM flight to Nice. Dragging herself out of bed to the bathroom, she stepped into the shower. Letting the cool water run through her hair, stream down onto her face, she tried to rinse away her lethargy and thoughts of Jeremy.

Racing to make her flight, Natalie tossed her belongings into the suitcase. Before she placed her dress from last night in her bag, she held it close to her face trying to inhale the remnants of Jeremy's cologne. Despondent, she folded it carefully, set it in her valise, and zipped it shut.

Downstairs the concierge helped her into a taxi. On the way to the airport, Natalie passed the places she had walked by only hours ago with the man she loved. She was desolate—heartbroken by her own choosing. She knew that if she saw him again, she would not let him go.

At the airport while waiting to board the plane, Natalie reflected on the moment she and Jeremy first saw one another—his deep brown inviting eyes, his soft sultry voice, his arm around her back almost claiming her as his. She regretted settling for David when she could be with someone who felt passion for her. Once seated on the plane and in the air, Natalie stared hopelessly at the thin white clouds, reflecting on the eight-hour conversation she had shared with her soul mate over the ocean.

After arriving in Cannes, she checked into the Carlton on *Boulevard de la Croisette*. When she settled in her room, Natalie opened her palm pilot to look up Enrique Santiago's private line. She was going through the motions of daily life without paying any mind to the details. She was distracted, absorbed in missing Jeremy. She dialed the phone.

"Enrique, please."

She was put on hold.

"My secretary said there is a woman with an American accent on the telephone," Santiago said. "Natalie, my little pinch hitter, how are you? And how is that lazy ass boss of yours?"

"We're fine, Enrique," she said with all the energy she

could muster.

"In all seriousness, I know I am in good hands, Natalie. My son and I will meet you at your hotel at seven. Tell me, where are you staying?"

"The Carlton."

"Glad to hear your company's outrageous fees are keeping you comfortable… It excites me to give a beautiful woman a hard time. Please forgive me... We'll talk over drinks and dinner and then you'll make both my son and I look like two Don Juans by allowing us to escort you to our 100th anniversary party."

"I wouldn't miss it, Enrique. I'll see you then."

When Natalie hung up the phone, she walked to the window overlooking the beach. She thought how great it would be to stroll along the promenade with Jeremy—her hand in his. She craved to hear his soft voice utter her name, to look into his cavernous eyes, to kiss his warm, tender lips again. As Natalie put her organizer back in her bag, she saw the card Jeremy had given her. She dialed the number of his residence in an impetuous moment.

"You've reached the voice mail of Jeremy Dalton. I'm away at the moment but will return your call if you leave a message..."

Natalie pressed the receiver down when she heard the beep. She didn't know what to say. She felt a small measure of comfort hearing the sound of his voice. Exhausted from not having slept much in the last day and a half, she set the alarm by the bed for 6 PM, falling into a deep sleep thinking of her soul mate.

When the buzz and bleep of the alarm woke her, Natalie groggily shambled to the bathroom to splash cool water on her sleepy face. After patting it dry with the plush white towel, she touched up her make up so that she would not look drained. She pulled her hair into an upswept do with combs to accentuate the burgundy velvet décolleté evening dress she slipped on that hugged her svelte, slender physique. Wispy ringlet curls dangled onto her shoulders framing her angelic face and alabaster neck.

The phone rang. Natalie wished it were Jeremy. But on this excursion he had not heard her tell the taxi driver her destination as he had in Paris.

"We're here," Enrique said. "We'll be in the lounge on the main level waiting patiently for you."

"See you in a minute," she said.

Natalie fastened a pearl and ruby choker around her neck, slipped into her burgundy velvet pumps and whisked out the door. She looked as though she had stepped out of another century. Elegant. When she entered the lounge, she was escorted to Santiago's table in the center of a majestically decorated room. Light shone in through a large picture window. Oversized paintings of cliffside landscapes lined the forest green walls.

"Natalie, you are as exquisite as I remembered from my last trip to

New York," Enrique said. "This is my son, Juan Carlos." They both stood to greet her.

"As always, it is good to see you Enrique and it's a pleasure to meet the young man who is going to take over your empire," Natalie said, extending her hand to Juan Carlos.

"Why don't we get the business out of the way so we can enjoy the rest of the evening?" Enrique asked.

"Sounds good," Natalie replied. "Pete brought me up to speed before I left. I understand you're selling off your consumer electronics division to focus on your core business and you want Stevens Worth Aikens to handle the sale for Santiago Enterprises."

"That's correct and tonight I am announcing that my son will be taking the helm at the beginning of our next fiscal year."

"Which is September," Natalie added.

"Yes and we want the sale completed by then, so the sooner we can take care of this…"

"We already have an interested potential buyer."

"Music to my ears… tell me who."

"It's an investment group—a consortium of American venture capitalists looking for a place to stow a wad of cash off shore for a few years and watch it grow from a distance."

"Well, if they are Americans, they should be able to afford our asking price."

"Pretty close but they will want some housekeeping items thrown in."

"Like?"

"They want you to do a ten percent layoff of the factory working staff worldwide before the sale is announced and then to stay on in a consulting capacity for one year so there is continuity and the remaining executive ranks don't jump ship. Gotta dress it up for 'the Street' you know."

Throughout dinner, the three continued their discussion of the details surrounding the demands of the potential buyer and positioning their response. Focusing her thoughts on business was a temporary distraction from the memory of Jeremy. After their meal, Natalie, Santiago, and Juan Carlos shuffled into Santiago's limousine waiting in the circular driveway outside the entrance to the Carlton. The winding drive along the picturesque coast to Santiago's villa captivated her attention.

Wedged into the light-speckled hills, the villa was surrounded by an ornate electronic gate that swung open as they drew closer. Commanding Italian spruces lined the extended driveway leading to the front of Enrique's elaborate home. On the approach, from a short distance, they could hear the din of the crowd and festivities. The limousine dropped them at the front entrance—Corinthian pillars to the left and right of twelve-foot doors sporting lion-faced knockers. Italian marble gleamed on the floor of the foyer. Santiago led Natalie on his arm to a grand hall, mirrors in all directions, enormous crystal chandeliers hung from a ceiling that was painted with pastoral scenes of frolicking nymphs. A throng of guests whirled about the reception that was well underway in this magical palace. The sound of Mozart and violins beckoned them forward. Juan Carlos followed dutifully behind.

A constant stream of well-wishers welcomed Santiago. Natalie stayed glued to his side while he scurried her around as if she were a trophy, introducing her to all his business cronies. She took every opportunity to sell the investment banking services of Stevens Worth Aikens. Natalie doled out requested business cards like a black jack dealer in Las Vegas. This was a potpourri of opportunity. Her anticipated services were in high demand along with views of her cleavage. In the midst of conversation, Natalie fell silent. She thought she saw Jeremy across the ballroom. Her heart began to race, her face grew pale. Then he was gone. Wishful thinking she thought, her mind playing tricks. Had she imagined him in the distance?

"Enrique, who is this beautiful woman that you have obviously been hiding from me?" a sultry voice coming from behind Natalie asked. She was startled for a moment by the familiar tone.

"Natalie, I would like you to meet my long-standing business associate, friend, and rival, Jeremy Dalton," Santiago said.

She turned to face Jeremy not believing that it was him. She was secretly elated to see him, but puzzled. How did he end up at this gathering and how did he know her boss' biggest client?

"You are too kind, Enrique. Actually, Natalie and I are very well acquainted. No need for formal introductions. Are you boring this exquisite lady to bits by introducing her to all your cigar smoking comrades?" Jeremy asked.

"That has not been my intent. We've been discussing business matters…"

"Sorry to interrupt, but they're ready for you to make your speech," Juan Carlos said.

"Please excuse me. I trust you will be in good hands, Natalie, with my colleague," Enrique said.

"Aaahh… destiny…" Jeremy said, kissing Natalie's hand.

Her cheeks were aching from the enormous smile she fashioned just seeing him again.

"You look… mmmm… good enough to eat. I want to start at the back of your delicate neck, nibbling my way down, up, and around again."

She beamed in response to his flattery.

"I am not letting you go this time, Natalie," he said. "Meeting here again… we are meant to be together. I am not taking this encounter lightly. There is a higher power at play here greater than we are."

She was entranced by his presence and the sound of the music in the background. "It's a Viennese," she said. "The waltz is my most favorite dance."

Jeremy extended his arm to her. "Shall we?" he asked.

"Are you sure you want to do this? Do you really know how? I wouldn't want to ruin my reputation," she joked.

"Well, we'll just have to see, now won't we?"

They walked closer to the sound of the music, the room adjacent to the ballroom. Natalie's playful concerns were more than allayed. Jeremy navigated the Italian marble smoothly, without flaw. The room spun while they sailed rhythmically around the dance floor. She felt like Cinderella and the man she danced with her Prince Charming. When the music stopped, they stood breathless staring into each other's eyes—hearts pounding. The musicians were taking a break so that Santiago could address his guests. Natalie and Jeremy lingered on the dance floor in the deafening silence holding one another. Everyone had made his or her way into the grand ballroom to hear Enrique.

"I could stand here like this with you all night... Perhaps we should get a drink," Jeremy suggested.

They maneuvered through the crowd to the bar in the back of the room by the oversized French doors leading to the terrace.

"Two Perriers with lime, please" he requested.

She chuckled to herself, tickled that he remembered what she liked to drink.

The bartender passed them their beverages in champagne glasses.

"It's a little warm in here," Jeremy said. "You gave me quite a workout. Would you care to join me on the verandah for a breath of cool night air?" he asked in a mockingly formal tone.

He led her outside.

"Aaahh… we're alone," he said, leaning against the mini-pillared railing. He watched Natalie jubilantly peering over the balustrade with the excitement of a wide-eyed child gazing in awe at the panorama that engulfed them. The city lights of Cannes twinkled in the distance. The aroma of the sea filled the air as the waves crashed energetically below them.

"This view is amazing," she said.

"Not as amazing as mine," Jeremy said, pulling Natalie close so that her body pressed against his. He kissed her passionately, frantically exploring every crevasse of her sweet-tasting mouth. His hands ran wildly over her taut body, caressing what lay beneath the velvet dress.

She lost herself in him. She could not stop. This felt right, the way love was supposed to be. Natalie could not conjure a single thought of David as she had before when she was with Jeremy. She unleashed herself, reciprocating his passion, kissing him in an ecstatic frenzy. "I know you are where I'm supposed to be," she said between kisses while her fingers ran through his silken hair then over his rounded hard pecs. Natalie pulled Jeremy closer to her. He pressed himself into her. She could feel his hardness on her hip. They could not stop.

"I have to have you, Natalie... I want to... make love to you... all night... under the stars," he said almost gasping for air in between nibbling and stroking her.

Natalie sighed and moaned softly like a contented purring kitten.

"Tell me... you want me... as much... as I want you," he said.

"Take me... I'm yours... Somehow I think I always have been," she said.

Inside, Santiago was standing on a raised platform addressing his two hundred guests. Through the glass doors they heard a muffled version of his announcement.

"Friends, tonight marks a very special occasion and I thank you for being here to share it with me," Enrique said. "I have some good news and some great news. First, the good news... I will remain as Chairman of Santiago Enterprises. The great news is that I will be stepping aside as President and CEO and will be passing the torch to my immensely capable son, Juan Carlos, whom you all know..."

"I want to be in you. I want to ravage your body. We can't stay here," Jeremy said. "I have an idea. Don't move." He pulled himself reluctantly away from her supple lips and roaming hands. Jeremy crept back inside. All eyes were on Santiago. Jeremy snuck upstairs to the bedroom above the terrace where Natalie waited anxiously.

"Hey, beautiful," he whispered from the window above her.

"What are you doing up there?" she asked.

"Catch." He tossed a comforter he had taken off of a bed down to her.

"I think you've gone mad," she said.

"I'm mad for you, that's all," he said. "Be right down." He again tiptoed passed the festivities to return to Natalie.

Like teenagers sneaking out after curfew, they descended the winding stone stairway off the verandah that led to the parking area. Within a few minutes of hunting, they stumbled upon Jeremy's black Porsche. He drove to the beach they saw from the terrace, aggressively shifting and revving the engine. His fancy maneuvering excited Natalie. He screeched into a dead stop, parking with the tail of the vehicle sticking out at an angle from the curb. He turned off the engine.

"Are you going to leave the car like this?" Natalie asked.

"Ah, it's just a car," he replied jokingly. "It'll be fine. Everyone parks that way around here." He stepped out of the car and jogged around to Natalie's door to help her out. "Come on, my little love goddess," he said, taking her hand as she got up. Jeremy carried the blanket in his other hand.

When he slammed the door shut behind them with his hip, it resonated in Natalie's head a dozen times. She felt as though she was shutting the door on her life, as she knew it. Each step forward on the sand-sprinkled street was distancing her from David and their future together. Natalie removed her burgundy pumps to walk on the beach hoisting one side of her gown up so that it wouldn't drag.

Jeremy fanned the comforter through the air. They watched it billow and settle in anticipation of consuming one another. She tossed her shoes aside. He took off his jacket, bola, and then slowly unbuttoned his crisp white shirt while Natalie hungrily watched. Jeremy's tan skin looked smooth and inviting. His bare chest tantalized her. Jeremy turned her so they were both facing the lightly rippling water and began kissing the back of her neck. He sent her instantly into a dream-like state. Her eyes rolled back in her head. She caressed his cheek with her hand while he unzipped her dress. Her gown dropped to the ground. Natalie stood wearing only a black sheer thong. Her rounded, pert breasts were at attention, beckoning Jeremy.

"Good lord, you are amazing, Natalie. How did I get this lucky?" He took a deep breath. "I'm totally head over heels in love with you... I mean it... Once I have you... I know that's gonna be it... I won't be able to share you..." He held her face in his hands and leaned his forehead against hers. "Please tell me you're mine."

"Nothing, no one can compare to you, to being with you. I'm totally in love with you. Take me... I'm yours..."

He knelt down onto the crimson and gold satin blanket extending his hand to Natalie helping her to join him. He leaned over to her and delicately kissed her lips and breasts. She pulled him into her as they fell slowly back onto the cool cloth beneath them. He kicked off his shoes from his sockless feet. She opened his belt and trousers and peeled them off along with his tight black underwear. Jeremy tore her thong off with his teeth. They both lay naked before one another like two animals in the wild, free to explore the passion they felt at their core.

Jeremy charged into her like a bull meets its prey. Natalie slithered under him like a stealthy asp. Their bodies danced with one another in consummate harmony. He lunged into her. She gasped with ecstasy. He rode her forcefully. They were undulating and arching in concert with the universe. She pulled him closer into her screaming, moaning with ecstatic rapture, surrendering herself to him completely. He grunted and groaned as he masterfully pleasured both himself and Natalie simultaneously. No man had done that for her before. Jeremy lay draped over Natalie, spent. She was in another world enjoying the reverberations of their lustful play. He remained inside her until they were capable of moving or thinking. They were adhered to one another.

"I could be with you forever," Jeremy whispered.

"Don't let this moment end," Natalie replied.

"It doesn't have to. Stay with me, Natalie. We could make love day and night."

She flipped them over onto their sides. Natalie stroked Jeremy's face looking into his deep brown eyes. "There is nowhere on earth I would rather be than with you," she said.

He pulled out of her slowly kissing her lovingly. He stood up and pulled her up with him gently. They frolicked in the water splashing each other, kissing, while the moonlight's reflection on the surf danced around them. They played in the gentle waves until their skin was wrinkled, prune-like, and Natalie's teeth began to chatter. Dripping wet, they ran, naked, back to the blanket and wrapped themselves. They lay nestled into one another, cuddling until the first hint of dawn. Natalie and Jeremy watched the sun come up over the horizon caressing each other.

"I love you, Natalie," he said, cupping her face in his hands.

"What took you so long to find me?" Natalie asked. "I feel like I've waited my whole life for you."

"Maybe I've been right in front of you the whole time but you weren't ready to see me."

Before the sun was fully up and all the early morning beachcombers were out and about, Natalie and Jeremy dressed themselves after their night of passion. She slipped her velvet dress back on fumbling with the zipper.

"Here. I've got it," he said, tenderly kissing the back of her neck. He pulled on his pants and crinkled shirt.

"I can't imagine what I look like right now," Natalie said. "My hair is probably going in a million different directions."

"I think you look sexy… and satisfied," he said grinning.

"Oh, we sure are cocky early in the day," she said kidding.

As they walked through the cool sand back to his car, Jeremy put his arm around her and kissed the side of her head. "I know, but isn't that one of the things you love about me?"

They got into Jeremy's car to go to the Carlton to collect Natalie's things, driving along the winding roads that had looked so magical the night before. When they arrived at the hotel, the doorman greeted them.

"Checking in?" he asked, opening Natalie's door in his Napoleonic-type outfit.

"Actually, checking out," she replied.

They left the car in the circular driveway while they went to her room. Jeremy mauled Natalie in the elevator.

"You know they have cameras in here for guys like you," she said laughing.

"I can't keep my hands off you in public so why should I in private?" he quipped.

"You know you have a point," she replied walking down the corridor.

"Nice shack they have you in here," Jeremy said when she opened the door to her suite. He walked over to the window. "View of the beach. Not bad for a little girl from the 'burbs.'"

"How did you know I'm from the 'burbs?'" she asked while brushing her hair.

"Well… uh… I just figured a young lady such as yourself with all your obvious good societal grooming would probably have grown up in suburbia. Am I right?" he asked agitatedly.

"Lucky guess, I suppose," she said, rummaging through her bag. "I better call Santiago and let him know I made it back to the hotel unscathed and tidy up a few loose ends with him before we head out." Natalie pulled her cell phone out of her handbag and dialed his private line again.

A male voice answered.

"Enrique, please."

"Natalie, is that you?" Enrique asked. "You had me worried. Are you okay?"

"Yes. I'm fine. Your colleague, Jeremy Dalton, was nice enough to see me home. I didn't want to disrupt you and spoil your celebration last night so we ducked out quietly after your speech." She walked into the bathroom, closed the door and turned the faucet on at the sink. "On a business note, I will bring Peter up to speed about everything we discussed.

We'll try and reel in this investor group for you and wrap up the deal as neatly and quickly as possible. We think the terms they're suggesting are within reason given that your asking price is a little inflated so I would strongly consider their proposal. Let Pete know next week what your thoughts are," she said, turning off the running water. "Thanks for dinner, a wonderful party, and a whole lot more..." she said, walking out of the bathroom toward Jeremy. She reached for his hand.

"Natalie, always a pleasure seeing you and working with you and besides, you have nicer legs than your boss. We'll talk soon."

"Such the business woman, making sure your conversation can't be overheard..." Jeremy put his arms around Natalie and pressed his forehead against hers. "Do you... not trust me?" he asked, looking into her eyes and then kissed her slowly.

"It's not a matter of trust... It's protecting client confidentiality... Should I... not trust you?" she asked and then kissed him back sensually nibbling on his lips.

Jeremy swooped her up, laid her on the bed, and then straddled her, pinning her down. "I think you should, Angel," he said.

Natalie became immediately distracted. Her mind returned to a time long ago... to a time when sex was about violence and pain instead of love... She closed her eyes and held her hands over her face. "Stop!" she screamed.

Jeremy pulled her hands away and held her head. "It's okay. It's okay," he said in a soothing tone.

She opened her eyes. Her breathing was ragged. She pushed Jeremy off of her and got up from the bed.

Chapter Five

"What happened?" Jeremy asked as Natalie stepped out of the vanity area of the bathroom drying her hair with a towel.

I don't want to talk about it," she replied. Natalie threw her belongings in the suitcase and she and Jeremy returned to his car. Natalie was shaken from the memory of her rape.

While they drove in silence, Jeremy had a fire in his eyes.

Natalie was certain he was angry and hurt that she had rejected him. She did not want to explain it wasn't him.

After forty-five minutes, they came to a quaint town with small shops and outdoor cafes with colorful awnings. Natalie noticed Jeremy's searing look melt away.

"I can't wait to share this with you," he said. While at a stop sign, he took her hand and placed a delicate kiss on her palm. "This is where I go to get away from civilization." He turned the car onto a steep hill that led down to the beach. The house was tucked away amid old majestic trees and was situated on a small, secluded bay. Jeremy parked the car in an overgrown driveway that looked like it had not been manicured in years.

Natalie reached for her bags getting out of the car.

"Let me get those," he said.

The warm three-bedroom bungalow had a large living room with a masonry brick fireplace, vaulted ceiling, and a tiny bachelor-styled kitchen. Exotic colorful paintings covered the walls. Statues, sculpture, and other three-dimensional art decorated the end tables, mantel, and coffee table.

"You have to come and see the view." Jeremy raised the ceiling-to-floor wooden blinds opening the sliding glass doors that led to the red clay-tiled deck. The rays of sunshine drenched the tiny inlet forcing Natalie to squint as she soaked in nature's beauty. The water rippled gently against the rocks that jutted out from the shore.

"Why don't you unpack and settle in," Jeremy said. "I'm starving after last night. I'll run across the street and pick up some fresh fruit, bread, cheese, and other goodies to fix us a breakfast feast. I want to ensure that I keep up my energy so that I can ravage you again and again—if you'll let me. I want you to feel comfortable here. Just let me know whatever you need. Your wish is my command... The extremely handsome, charming, and very humble Jeremy Dalton is at your service, ma lady," he said mockingly on one knee. "I feel badly about what happened this morning. I don't ever want to do anything that makes you uncomfortable."

She hugged him. "Thank you," Natalie said with a heartfelt tone. "I feel better just being here with you."

"I'll be back before you know it," Jeremy said. "We can picnic outside and make love until sunset. Then we'll have a romantic candlelit dinner and make love until dawn and start all over again tomorrow."

"Are there any other activities on the agenda beside eating and sex?" she asked playfully.

"No," he replied emphatically.

"You seem pretty certain."

"If you have any ideas you can submit them to the committee for review."

"Let me guess... you are the committee."

"You are truly brilliant," he said and planted a loud kiss on the top of her head. "See you soon, baby." He turned abruptly and headed to the store.

She walked back into the house and stood in the center of the living room. Natalie turned around in a circle to soak in her environment looking for any memorabilia that would help her get to know further the man she loved. But there was nothing of any personal nature. No photos, no bric-a-brac, not a single item with history of any kind.

When Jeremy returned, Natalie was clad in a white Brazilian-cut bathing suit lounging on the deck.

He placed his sacks on the kitchen counter and walked outside to her. "Lord, have mercy on my soul," he said, watching Natalie sun worship. He sat down next to her on the chaise. "Screw, breakfast. I don't need food. Just you," he said, kissing and nibbling on her neck.

"Well, I need you... and food," she said, pulling herself up making a dash for the kitchen.

He lingered on the lounger bewilderedly tickled with her child-like tease.

Natalie rummaged through the parcels to see what he had bought. "*L'Entretien*," she said, reading from the outside of one of the bags.

"That's the name of the little grocery store up the street," he said. The little old woman who owns the place watches over the house when I'm not here. It's like having a French grandmother. She says I remind her of her husband who died like forty years ago. She's very sweet but... not as sweet as you," he said, lifting Natalie up onto the counter. Jeremy wrapped her legs around him kissing her deeply and passionately satiating an abysmal hunger. He quickly cleared all the groceries away and hovered over Natalie on the cold ceramic-topped island.

She responded to him eagerly by ripping off his shirt and running her warm soft hands frantically over his tanned smooth back. They made love tirelessly. Jeremy's stamina pleasured Natalie over and over again. She delighted in his rhythmic, masculine prowess. She could not catch her breath.

When he reached his climax, he thrust into her with the power of a thousand oceans rendering her into a deeper state of ecstasy.

A short time later, they satisfied their physical hunger, gorging on the sumptuous treats that Jeremy had bought. After, they napped lying on a white blanket spread over the fire hot sand—both exhausted from their night and morning of passion together. Simply knowing Jeremy was by her side enabled Natalie to fall into a deep, nurturing, and healing sleep. When the blazing sun began to fall behind the sweeping trees adjacent to the house, Natalie was woken by goose bumps forming on her arms and legs from the coolness in the air. She turned over onto her side to look at Jeremy. He was blissfully sleeping. Natalie stroked his unshaven face slowly wondering what he was dreaming about and how lucky she felt to be there with him. Jeremy started to waken.

"Hi," he said. "Were you watching me sleep?"

"No. I was just checking to see if you were still breathing," Natalie said giggling. "It's actually next Thursday. You've been asleep quite a while."

"If it were next Thursday, would I be here alone?" he inquired.

Natalie was silent. She turned looking away from him. "I don't know how to answer that," she replied.

"Would you stay if I asked?"

"It would depend on the context of what you were really asking."

That night they made a fire and watched it burn while sipping a dry Chardonnay and sitting on throw pillows on the floor in front of the fireplace. The shadows cast by the flames danced whimsically across their faces as Natalie and Jeremy stared into each other's eyes. The sound of the crackling of the wood echoed in the background of their impassioned sighs as Jeremy made magical love to Natalie again.

"Don't stop," she murmured breathlessly.

Natalie and Jeremy enveloped one another. His limbs were entwined around hers, an octopus clutching its dinner prey. They brought each other to the edge of ecstasy until together they surrendered, succumbing to their own inner Eden.

Under the stars, they showered in an open-air cedar closet off the back of the house. They slathered each other up and down with soap, making amusing shapes with the shampoo bubbles. They were laughing and loving each other. The spray of the tepid water kept them only modestly warm. Natalie's breasts, adorned with alluring tan lines, were round and hard at full attention. She was shivering when Jeremy turned off the water.

He wrapped them in an oversized fluffy white towel, holding her close.

They crawled into bed together. Natalie felt secure, protected in Jeremy's muscular arms under the billowing and puffy white comforter. They lay on their sides, Jeremy's body cupping Natalie's sleek, slender shape. The rhythm of their breathing became a synchrastic ebb and flow of life as they drifted off peacefully to sleep.

Throughout the next three days, they made love every way imaginable—when they rose by the light of day under the covers, in the marble-tiled shower, on the sun-heated sand in the afternoon, and at night by a roaring fire. Their hunger for one another was unyielding. Natalie felt whole for the first time in her life. Jeremy's attention, caring, and soulfulness melted the invisible emotional wall Natalie had erected after always being hurt in her relationship with David.

In between their lovemaking, Natalie and Jeremy probed each other's intellect and psyche, sharing their most private fears, hopes, and beliefs. They had more in common than she could have imagined. They liked the same art, literature, movies, even the same flavor of ice cream. Was it 'soulmatehood' or coincidence?

On Natalie's last night before she was to return home she checked for messages on her cellular telephone. Jeremy was sitting outside on the wooden deck on the lounge staring up at the stars. After she listened to her calls, Natalie lay down with her back toward him and also gazed up at the twinkling dots in the sky. He clutched her tightly in his arms as they were both sprawled on the chaise.

"What's going to happen to us tomorrow?" Jeremy asked. "I am completely in love with you. I want to spend the rest of my life with you, Natalie."

"I can't bear the thought of leaving you," she said. "I don't want to talk about it. I feel like this has been the most amazing dream. I never want it to end." Her greatest fear was losing her soul mate now that she thought she had found him.

"It doesn't have to end, Natalie." Jeremy took her hand standing up and led her down the three steps to the sand. He perched himself on one knee, looking up at her. Natalie's mane wafted lightly in the soft bay breeze. She ran her fingers through his waves of silken hair.

"Spend eternity with me... marry me, Natalie." Waiting for her response, he placed his head on her stomach and stared out at the water.

She stroked his head. She knelt down to look into his eyes. "I want to be with you forever."

"All we need is you... me... and God. We don't need a fancy party with lots of people we don't even like.... We can just..."

"I agree..."

Jeremy reached for both her hands. They looked into each other's eyes.

"I, Jeremy Robert, pledge to you Natalie..."

"Anne."

"...my undying, eternal love. I promise to cherish you and be devoted only to you until death parts us. You are my soul mate now and forever." He took off the gold cross that was hanging on a chain around his neck and placed it around Natalie's neck over the cross and chain she was wearing.

"I, Natalie Anne, promise to love you, Jeremy Robert and be faithful to you until death parts us. My love for you will come before all other commitments. You, too, are my soul mate for eternity. I will always love only you." She removed her necklace and placed it on Jeremy. They hugged each other tightly, almost fusing as one. Jeremy felt a tear drop onto his shoulder. He pulled away enough to confirm that Natalie was crying. He wiped her tears.

"I still need to go tomorrow," she said and began to sob.

"You don't have to leave. Please. I need you to be with me..."

"I don't want to leave, but I checked my voice mail earlier and my boss is angry at me because my clients aren't happy with the guy who's working with them while I'm gone. And I got a message from my father. He's infuriated that my sister is doing all the work for my... I didn't want to tell you and ruin..." She stopped herself from going further when she saw him grimace with hurt.

"What are you saying?"

"I'm saying that I need to go back and end that relationship, cancel a wedding, give notice at my job, and create a plan with you to come back so that we can be together."

"I'll go back with you. I've got commitments here, but it's worth it to me to have a life with you."

"It's not right for me to ask you to do that," Natalie said.

"You're doing it all over again. I'm not good enough for you."

"What do you mean again?" she asked.

"I didn't mean... again. I'm just upset that's all," he said flustered. "Natalie, stay with me here... in paradise. If you go back, you won't return. You'll get sucked up back into your old life. People would kill for the type of connection we have. Don't do this to us."

"I just pledged to spend the rest of my life with the man I am totally in love with. I just need to undo some things at home to be with you for eternity. I'm thinking a month max and we'll be back together. I can put some feelers out with my clients here and try and line up a new job."

"You don't need to work at all if you don't want to. I can take care of you financially."

"I enjoy my work and my financial independence. It's who I am."

"No it's not. It's what you do. There's a difference."

"So, what are you saying? You're a 'kajillianaire' and I don't need to pull my weight or… we'll just live on love?"

"If that was a multiple choice, the answer is 'A.'"

"Come on," she said. "Be serious."

"I am being totally serious. Am I good enough for you now, Princess?" he said in a condescending angry tone.

Natalie grabbed her head and dropped to the ground. Thoughts of her rape suddenly flooded her mind. "Stoooop!" she screeched.

Jeremy picked her up in his arms and carried her to the bed they had been sharing. He held her close.

Natalie clung to him for comfort. She was shaken.

"It's okay," he said in a soothing tone patting her head. "I'm so sorry we fought. I don't want to hurt you, baby. I never wanted to hurt you." They held each other until they drifted into a restless slumber.

Chapter Six

The following morning Jeremy awoke before dawn. Quietly he put on his clothes that lay on the floor next to the wooden poster bed while Natalie slept peacefully. Jeremy leaned over and kissed the side of her head.

"Good-bye, Princess. You'll always be my one and only angel," he whispered in her delicate ear.

Natalie began to stir. Nightmares began running wildly through her mind. She was in a forest-like area with a faceless man standing over her and beating her with a large stick. She was bleeding from her head and her vagina. Tossing and thrashing, she reached out to Jeremy for comfort. Her eyes fluttered open. He was not there. His side of the bed was cold. She sat up startled.

"Jeremy?" she called out.

There was no answer.

Natalie swung her legs out from under the bed covers, placed her feet on the night-chilled floor and crept into the living room. Her beloved was not there. She returned to the bedroom and poked her head in the darkened bathroom. No sign of him. His razor, cologne, tooth brush—all the toiletries he had been using were gone. Natalie opened the bedroom closet door. The hangars that had held his suits, shirts, and pants were barren. She ran to the front door to find it ajar. Wearing Jeremy's t-shirt, Natalie walked outside gingerly stepping over tiny white pebbles. Jeremy's car was no longer in the driveway. The leaves of the trees rustled in the cool morning air. Natalie's hair snapped in her face from the wind whipping at her. She stood alone and perplexed, trying to collect her racing thoughts.

Cold and bewildered she went back inside to locate her cell phone to see if there were any new messages. There were none. She called the telephone numbers on the business card he had given her. She heard messages saying that she had dialed an invalid number for all that were listed. She lifted the receiver of the telephone on the kitchen wall. There was no dial tone. The line was dead. She walked out onto the deck. The small drop of wine in each of the goblets from the night before was almost dried to the bottom of the glasses. She felt for Jeremy's chain and cross that he had placed around her neck hours early. By clutching the necklace, Natalie felt a measure of relief from the sick panic settling in her gut.

She frantically tore apart the living room and kitchen looking for a note from Jeremy, searching in every nook and crevice, but there was nothing. Returning to the bedroom, looking on the dresser, again, nothing. She pulled the comforter off the bed and swept it through the air. Nothing. Nothing. Nothing. Natalie hastened to pull on a pair of shorts, her sandals, and sunglasses and walked to town. She found *L'Entretien*, the small grocery store Jeremy had shopped at days earlier. Behind the register was a frail, elderly lady Natalie hoped was the 'French grandmother' Jeremy spoke of. Natalie prayed the old woman might know where he was. Maybe in leaving he might have stopped at the store to let her know to watch the house, she thought.

"Pardon, Madame. Est-ce que vous êtes le propriétaire? Natalie asked.

"Oui."

"Connaissez-vous Jeremy Dalton?"

"Qui?"

The old woman was the owner but did not know Jeremy. Natalie described him to her and reminded her that she watched his house for him when he was away. The ancient, wrinkled face was vacant. She told Natalie she must be thinking of someone else.

On her slow despondent walk back to the house, Natalie started to cry, afraid, not understanding what had happened. Did the man who said he loved her more than anyone ever had before abandon her like a stray kitten, she thought to herself. She could not know with certainty his reason for leaving without him telling her. Perhaps he was suddenly called away for business. Maybe the deal he was in the middle of in Paris soured and unexpectedly needed his immediate attention. She could only guess. But the phone had not rung during the night or early morning.

Knowing she was to return to Paris to fly home, the man she thought she knew would have waited to spend every precious last minute of their time together. Natalie wondered if he did not believe she would return to him and did not feel her sincerity about being together for eternity. Had she hurt him too deeply? Irreparably? This possibility above all others gnawed at the inner lining of her stomach. But she had meant it. Natalie planned to return. She hated herself for leaving any room for Jeremy to feel doubt in any way. But she still needed to make an appropriate transition to her new life. She could not just stay on indefinitely cocooned from the world. But in Jeremy's mind, she thought, maybe that was what he was truly asking her to do. These thoughts spun through her head circulating like whirlpools at the base of Niagara Falls—crashing between the walls of her skull. She wept ceaselessly on her walk, not caring who saw her sobbing relentlessly, wiping her tears on her shirt.

When she returned to the house, Natalie went out to the beach, reliving their lovemaking in her mind. Then she fell to the ground, holding her face in her hands while the tears poured down her cheeks like rain in a thunderstorm. For Natalie, the most disturbing, unsettling thought was that there was no remnant of him—no trace that Jeremy had ever been there—apart from the two empty, now ghost-like, wine glasses. Tormented, Natalie prayed Jeremy would return before she would have to leave for the airport in Nice. But he did not.

Natalie frantically showered and chaotically threw her things in her bag so that she could get off the train in Cannes to see if he was at the business address on his card. With her hair still wet, she dragged her luggage through town to the train station. Standing on the platform, Natalie was numb, staring off at nothing at all, emotionally crippled from pain. In a daze, she boarded her train and disembarked two stops later in Cannes.

Wheeling her valise behind her, she reached in her jacket pocket and pulled out Jeremy's card to double check the address. She was familiar with the area and knew where *rue de la Montagne* was situated. Natalie found building 21 that was on Jeremy's card, but its windows were boarded up and the gate at the main entrance had a padlock on it. The building looked like it was abandoned. There was no sign that a viable business concern had been in operation there in any recent past. Desolate and confused, she looked at the card again—21 *rue de la Montagne*.

Natalie wound her way back to the train station. While walking through the charming streets lined with quaint cafes and exotic stores, nausea swept over her. As soon as she got inside the terminal, Natalie looked for a bathroom. She vomited until the queasiness in her stomach subsided. She rinsed her mouth out with cool water from the tap and wet her face. She looked up at the board to double check the track number and saw she had ten minutes until the departure time for the next train to Nice. Natalie reached into her pocketbook for her cell phone. She dialed her mother, desperately needing to hear a comforting voice.

"Hi, Mom. It's me," Natalie said in a scraggly tone, talking into an answering machine. She tried to clear her throat. "I'm on my way to the airport and just thought I would give you a call and let you know. I know it's early there. I guess you're sleeping if you're not picking up. Well, I'll be landing at JFK about seven tonight, your time. I'll give you a call when I get home."

The plane ride back seemed an eternity to Natalie. Staring out the window, she sat in a glazed stupor for eight hours of emotional torture, missing Jeremy, wounded by his disappearance. He said he loved her and wanted to spend his life with her last night and today he was gone… without a trace. She clutched the cross dangling from her neck while tears streamed down her ashen face. She did not eat. She barely moved. When the flight attendant spoke to her, she did not respond. She felt as though she wanted to die because life without her soul mate would be a living death. She had tasted love and felt what it was like to be loved for the first time.

When Natalie arrived in New York, to her surprise, her mother was there to meet her when she exited the customs and immigration doors. She was thankful and relieved to see her. When Natalie drew near, they reached out for one another. They embraced. Natalie wept uncontrollably. Her mother had known by the sound of her daughter's voice on the tape machine that she had been hurt—her heart broken—that she had loved and lost—the way only a mother could know. Natalie's mother stroked her hair, patting her head while she continued to sob, shaking.

"I know," her mother said in a soothing, nurturing tone. "It'll be all right. You're home now. You're going to be okay."

Somberly they walked to the car in silence with their arms linked. Her mother did not ask what had happened to her daughter. They settled into the car.

"Do you want to come home with me or should I drive you to your apartment?" her mother asked.

"I would rather go home with you, but I just don't want to deal with Daddy right now. And besides I've got to go to work tomorrow and would prefer not to have a near two-hour commute in the morning. Thank you though."

"I understand. The offer is there. Whatever you think is best, dear." Her mother held her hand.

They arrived in front of Natalie's apartment building. She leaned over and hugged her mother.

"Thank you, Mom," she said. "Thanks for not asking me…"

"Natalie, I love you. If you want to talk… about anything at all…" I can just listen," she said and let her daughter go.

Once in her apartment, Natalie put her luggage down and pressed the playback button on her answering machine. She had two messages.

"It's Adrian. Call me when you get back in. Mom said you went off on some business trip to France. Great time to be away, Nat. I have to go over some wedding details with you. Thank goodness you have me to take care of these decisions for you. By the way, you've got your final fitting this week, the florist can't get one of the flowers you want, and the caterers need to talk to you 'pronto' about the cake. God, one would think you had no interest in this…"

The machine beeped.

"Hey, Nat." It was David. "I think you're coming back today. Not totally sure. Call me when you get in. I had a great week. Have to tell you all about it."

There was no 'I missed you, Natalie. Can't wait to see you and hear all about your trip.' The thought of David sickened her. Now she knew love. What it felt like. What it tasted like. She longed for Jeremy. She checked her cell phone for messages, the only means Jeremy had to contact her. But there were none.

Natalie had thought she would no longer need Chuckles, her furry friend. But alone and sad, she crawled into her unmade bed with him for comfort. How could Jeremy just have walked away... out of her life... without a trace? He said he loved her but who was he really? Had he existed or did she want and need to feel loved so desperately that she had conjured him up. Natalie didn't know. She tortured and tormented herself, rolling these questions and thoughts through her mind, crying, hugging her teddy bear—sobbing until sleep conquered exhaustion and despair.

Chapter Seven

When the first glimmer of sunlight crept through Natalie's bedroom window, her eyes fluttered open. She reached over for Jeremy thinking, dreaming he was by her side. Natalie quickly realized she was alone. Tormented, she pulled herself together with every ounce of mental and physical energy she could muster to get ready for work. When she walked onto the trading floor and sat down at her desk, all of Natalie's colleagues were staring at her.

"Hey, Nashy," she said. "How did it go while I was out? Pete left me a message saying it was a little rough for you."

"Pete needs to see you, Nat," he said. "Where's my wine?"

"Shit." Natalie had forgotten.

"Guess not."

"Yeah. He said he needed to see you right away," Sue said.

"Welcome back."

Peter walked toward Natalie. "In my office," he demanded.

Natalie stood up and followed him back to his glass-enclosed office.

"Hope you had a nice, restful vacation," Peter said sarcastically. "What the fuck happened to my deal? I send in my ace and the whole thing falls apart. I need some answers, 'sweet meat.'"

"What the hell are you talking about? It was as good as done when I left," Natalie said.

"Don't play games with me."

"I can't answer you if I don't have the slightest clue what the hell you're talking about. Did you speak to Santiago?"

"What for? Why would I need to talk to Santiago if the deal is off?"

"What do you mean, it's off?"

"I got a call from the investor group saying they're not interested anymore and my lovely Senior Vice President would know why."

"I never had any contact with them."

"Well, my guy over at JRMD seems to know you and I have Enrique asking me a shit load of questions that I can't answer. So you better."

"I never had any contact with anyone at JRMD. Something is very fucked up here. Don't blame me, Pete, for ruining your deal when you should have been doing it yourself. I had nothing to do with it falling flat.

Maybe you need to go back to your buyer and ask him what his issues are. When I left Enrique, he was ready to sign on the dotted line. If you're that sure I did something wrong, then fire my ass. Oh, no wait... You can't afford to do that since I'm your biggest fucking revenue producer surrounded by all these fat house cats that sit around licking their fur all day. If you want to talk to me rationally, I'll be at the desk. So glad to be back."

Natalie turned around and walked out of Pete's office. When she sat down in her chair all the traders were glaring at her. They had heard her exchange with Peter.

"What are you all looking at? Don't you have work to do?" she said loudly to the crowd of nosy onlookers. Natalie noticed her message light was lit on her telephone console. She punched in her code to play the message.

"I'm very disappointed in you." It was Jeremy's voice. "I thought you would never leave me, Princess. I turn my back and you're gone. You didn't even wait to say good-bye. Is that how you treat someone you love?"

Natalie slammed the phone down. Her mind was flooded with a flash of an auditory memory of the day she was raped. The word 'princess' resonated in the echoes of her mind a thousand times. She grabbed her ears. Natalie wanted to scream, but was distracted by the frenzy of the activity in the market as it was picking up. Around her everyone was engaged in frantic transactions and heated telephone conversations that sobered her and brought her back to present day mentally. Natalie took a few deep breaths to collect her composure. No one had noticed her emotional turmoil. They were too involved in their own business to observe anything out of the ordinary.

When Natalie returned home that evening, her mother called to see how she was feeling after her tearful arrival the day before.

"Have you spoken to David since you've been back?" her mother asked.

"Not yet. He left a message but I can't bring myself to call him yet."

"I know it's none of my business but…"

"That's right, but go ahead because you will anyway."

They both laughed awkwardly.

"You were very upset when you got off the plane yesterday and I didn't want to make it worse. But there is little you don't know about your children when you're a mother… So I just want to ask… Do you love him?"

"Love who?"

"Natalie, please. I'm not talking about David."

Feeling uncomfortable about revealing her lack of fidelity to her mother, Natalie took a deep breath. She knew her mother was asking out of concern, not judgment.

"Yes, Mother. I do… or I did. When I got home I planned on telling David that it's over between him and me but…"

"And now, something has changed that?"

"A couple of bizarre things happened and I'm really not understanding what's going on…"

Natalie's father yanked the phone from her mother. "You're back finally," he said. "Good, because we're having a celebration tomorrow night at five o'clock at the office to congratulate David on making partner at the firm and I expect you to be there. And don't wear one of those tight or short skirts of yours like a prostitute. Dress like a lady for Christ's sake."

"Yes, Daddy. I'm fine. Thanks for asking."

"I know you're fine. You're mother would tell me if you weren't. Just make sure you're there tomorrow night to show support for your husband-to-be and all the hard work he does. Here's your mother."

"Sorry, dear. He grabbed the phone from me."

"Mother, I just don't know how you do it, but that's your choice I suppose."

"If I wasn't with your father, I wouldn't have you. That's the way I look at it and that's enough for me. You made it worth putting up with him. Anyway… I would be there tomorrow just for a little bit. Put in an appearance and then get a jet lag headache and leave early. You can still do whatever you want about the relationship later."

"I'll think about it."

Natalie decided to show up at the congratulatory party for David. When she arrived, Natalie walked into her father's office a few minutes before five and kissed him on his cheek.

"Hi, Daddy," she said.

"Always dressing like a whore. That's how your sister got knocked up. Is that what you want? I ask you to do one simple thing. Why should this be any different than when you were a teenager?"

David walked into Harv's office on the tail end of him lecturing Natalie.

"Hey, Nat. Did you hear the good news?" David asked.

"That's why I'm here."

David spent the evening gloating with his pompous colleagues while Natalie stayed in a corner distanced from the festivities wondering why he did not kiss her hello, or ask her when she got back, and why she hadn't called. After an hour she snuck out. Her absence went unnoticed by David and her father.

Chapter Eight

Natalie was disturbed that the deal fell through with Santiago. For her own peace of mind, she had to find a way to understand what transpired to cause Peter's buyer to pull their offer off the table. Early the next morning after David's congratulatory party, Natalie met with her boss for breakfast asking that he arrange a meeting with the key decision-makers from JRMD.

"Nat, I don't think they're going to agree to it," Peter said with strawberry jam on his cheek and corn muffin crumbs falling from his mouth.

"Well, isn't it worth a shot to try and resurrect this deal before it goes completely in the toilet?" she asked.

"You have a point." Peter pulled his cellular phone from the inside chest pocket of his suit coat and speed dialed a telephone number. While the call connected, he wiped the jam from his face. "Hey, Sally," he said. "Is JR there? It's Pete over at SWA."

"No," she said. "He's out of town. Cal Reynolds is handling all his calls while he's away. Would you like to speak with him?"

Pete was hesitant to answer.

"He's aware of the Santiago Enterprise deal," she said. "I'll put you through."

"Pete, I've been waiting for your call," Cal said when he picked up the phone. "I think my partner acted very impetuously to the high asking price of Santiago Enterprises in just walking away like that. He was pissed that your young S.V.P. didn't ask them to budge on it at all. There has to be some room for negotiation here."

"So you're saying you're still interested?"

"I am but I don't know about my partner."

"What do we have to do to make this happen?" Peter asked.

"JR wants to meet with this hot shot of yours privately to negotiate the terms of the agreement. Enrique is very impressed with her. JR wants her to do the deal. He'll be back in town tomorrow. Have her meet him at his hotel at six o'clock. He'll be staying at the Royale." Cal hung up.

"JR wants to meet with my young whippersnapper tomorrow night at his hotel," Peter said to Natalie. "That'd be you."

"Why just me? He's your client."

"I don't know. Just do it and don't screw it up. This is huge for the firm and my ass."

The following day, the market was extremely volatile and demanded Natalie's attention. By the time she came up for air at five o'clock, Peter
had already left the office. It occurred to her that she did not know what
JR looked like or where exactly she was to meet him at the hotel. Natalie
quickly grabbed her purse and Pete's file and nabbed a cab downstairs. She
arrived at the Royale at five minutes before six.

Natalie entered the ornately decorated, rococo lobby and sat in a big
oversized burgundy chair to rummage through Peter's Santiago Enterprises
folder to see if JR's last name was on any documents. It was not. Natalie
walked over to the attendant standing behind the reception desk. "Has anyone checked in under the firm name of 'JRMD?'" she asked the young
man.

"Let me have a look," he said. He fiddled with his computer key-
board a moment. "No. I'm sorry."

When Natalie turned back around, she saw Jeremy standing across
the golden-lit lobby watching her. She was stunned at the sight of him,
feeling paralyzed, unable to walk or make a move of any kind, thinking this
was another chance meeting. Their eyes locked. Jeremy began to walk
toward Natalie as if in slow motion. She edged closer to him without realizing her body was moving. She felt magnetically drawn to him. They
stood for what seemed to be an eternal moment staring into the depth of
each other's soul. Jeremy seemed different to Natalie, changed somehow.

101

His eyes were vacant and hard. She felt nervous to be near him. Her heart racing.

"I missed you," he said, breaking their silence.

Natalie wanted, needed to believe him. "Why did you leave me like that?" she asked, sounding child-like, feeling as though she were an abandoned kitten out in the rain though dressed in a high-powered Chanel business suit.

"I could ask you the same question," he replied coldly.

"You left me... in the middle of the night... no explanation... no good-bye. I thought you were staying in France for a few weeks."

"Things changed."

"Things changed for business?" Natalie asked.

"Yes, but mostly with us."

"What do you mean, with us?"

"I didn't come here to get into this right now," Jeremy said. "I'm here to discuss business."

"You're looking to meet up with a business associate here?" she asked.

"I'm here to meet with you."

"I thought you just said..."

"Natalie, I'm JR. I'm the consortium bidding for Santiago Enterprises."

"You bastard," she said, raising her hand in a burst of anger. She tried to slap Jeremy's face.

He grabbed her wrist in mid air and tamed her violence by kissing her soft palm and caressing her hand against his face. "I know you don't want to do that," he said.

"What the fuck do you know about what I want? You only got close to me because you knew I was..."

"People are looking. I didn't know you had such a fiery temper. You really are beautiful when you're mad," he said, taunting her.

"I don't care if people are looking," she said in a hushed tone, gritting her teeth. "You used me."

"How? I didn't ask you about the deal. Or try and get any information from you at all. Enrique doesn't even know who his potential buyer is at this moment. And your boss bailed on his own. We were put together by fate."

Natalie's wrath began to wane, her face more calm and angelic. "Even if all of that's true, this just all seems too coincidental."

"Maybe some of it, but it doesn't change the way we feel about one another. I still love you more than anything in the world."

"Then why did you leave?" Natalie asked.

"Because I really didn't think you would come back and I couldn't bear to say good-bye. I had to leave you, loving you not doubting you. It would have been too painful to lose you again."

"Again?"

Jeremy fidgeted and became awkward. "I mean... letting you go... like... at the airport in Paris," he stammered. "Why don't we go up to my suite and finish talking about this civilly, over a nice bottle of wine?"

The possibility of being close to him physically, privately, weakened her ability to further question his intent. She needed his love more than she needed answers that made complete sense.

Jeremy could see her emotional wall crumbling. He put Natalie's arm in his and led her to the elevator bank. He used a passkey to open a private lift to the penthouse. "I've missed your touch," he said, looking into her eyes as the elevator traveled up fifty floors. He pulled her against him and kissed her until the doors opened into a large, homey room with panoramic views of the city.

Natalie had begun to melt inside from his touch, from the smell of his cologne, the warmth of his skin. Her natural defenses and innate instincts were disarmed. "We really need to discuss the issues you have about Santiago Enterprises before we get completely sidetracked here. I need to reel this one in so let's just talk business for a minute," she said aware of herself, before losing all level-headedness.

"You're so businesslike and professional," he replied. "A woman who takes control. You're turning me on."

"Focus with me here. I'm not going to be able to do this for much longer unless we do this together," she confessed. "...The asking price is too high, your business partner said. Is that the issue?" she asked.

"No," he replied.

"No? Then what is?"

"I was angry you left."

"Holy shit. You mean to tell me you yanked your offer... Then why did you set up this meeting?"

"I had to see you again."

"This is freaking me out," Natalie said, backing away from Jeremy. "You would be doing this deal if I were not involved. Is that what you're saying?"

"Maybe. But you are here and that changes things."

"So now I walk into the office tomorrow and say… what...?"

"...That your investor group has agreed to Santiago's price. I don't want you to be angry with me. Right now I just need to make love to you. If that mean's dropping a few million in cash to do it then so be it." He walked around to the back of Natalie, lifted her thick mane of locks, and started to kiss her neck. "You're… worth… it," he said in between nibbles.

Natalie's mind told her to push him away and probe further to understand what was going on more fully. But her body did not want him to stop, and more importantly, neither did the little girl that dwelled within her who hungered for love and affection.

Jeremy unbuttoned her blouse slowly. He pushed her creamy white breasts up from under her brown lace bra and bit into them sensually.

Natalie ran her fingers through his silken hair, tugging at it passionately.

He removed her short-cropped jacket, matching mini skirt, and bra leaving them in a pile at her feet. She was left wearing a chocolate lace thong and four-inch Italian pumps. Jeremy led her to the king size bed and straddled her. He removed his tie, jacket, and shirt tossing them on the floor as Natalie watched. He leaned down kissing her hard, furiously, pinning her arms above her head. Their hands gripped one another, fingers spread open and then clasped tightly. Though his bottom half was clothed, Jeremy was thrusting his hips into Natalie, with penetrating force. Her pubic bone felt as though it were bruising. His belt buckle jammed into her stomach, digging into her skin. While kissing her feverishly, he bit her lip and then pinched her nipples.

"Aaahh," she winced.

Jeremy grabbed her face, kissing her harder than before.

She almost felt suffocated, unable to catch her breath. She gripped his hands trying to loosen them. He would not let go. Suddenly she felt his right hand release. Out of the corner of her eye, she saw him draw his arm back. Then his hand came crashing down on her face. Natalie's head spun sideways from the power of the blow. The skin on her cheek was on fire. Her ears rang. She turned in shock and looked up at Jeremy. She saw venom in his eyes.

"Don't... ever... leave... me," he whispered.

She was scared... and even more turned on.

In a flash of a second they were flipped over and Natalie was on top of Jeremy. She undid the belt that had been sticking her, removed his pants and tight black silk underwear. She kissed him with her back slightly arched. Her breasts, nipples erect, danced across his chest teasing him.

Jeremy was rock hard. From underneath her, he penetrated her and thrust himself deep within her. Natalie's head swung back, her spine tingled, her body shivered with pleasure as she rode him. Shock waves of ecstasy ran back and forth through them as if they were one. Her voice quivering, sighing, moaning breathlessly. His grunting low tribal tones told her he was on the verge of unleashing himself. She could not discern pleasure from pain.

Beads of his sweat drenched her body as they slid against one another. Her red nails scraped his back from top to bottom. He writhed when she pierced his skin but it heightened his passion. Digging in so hard, Natalie drew layers of skin and blood with her. As he came, he jammed himself into her so hard she screamed. She felt as though he released gallons of his juices in her as he continued to gyrate and gasp through multiple reverberations. When he was spent, he lay over her unable to move.

"You are fucking amazing," Jeremy said, trying to catch his breath. "No one can do that to me but you, baby. You drive me wild. Just the thought of you gives me a hard on. God, and being inside you... ah..."

Natalie had never been the object of so much passion. She basked in the afterglow, blanketed by his steaming body, loving the feeling that she could ignite a flame so great in someone. She craved for him to be in her again and again. She needed to feel loved, desired, more than she needed to know what happened to his phones or his business in Cannes.

"Stay with me tonight," Jeremy said. "I need you."

And she did. They raided the mini bar, drinking half of each of those tiny little bottles. They showered together in the double-headed marble stall. He pleasured her from behind as she leaned against the icy wall, screaming. He loved the way she looked with her long wet hair draping her back. Black mascara ran down her cheeks. She craved every inch of him.

After, Natalie and Jeremy ordered room service. They fed each other lobster, naked. Jeremy dipped the meat in butter and held it above Natalie until it began to drip down her chest. She reached for it. He put it in his mouth and she bit into it from his lips. He licked the slithery butter from her breasts. The cross he gave her dangled from her neck. Jeremy swigged LaFite from the bottle and passed it into Natalie's mouth from his. They made love, again, on the floor, to the sound effects of a pay-for-porn movie on the television in the background. Jeremy was rough, angry, as he moved in and out, biting her neck, pulling her hair. Natalie's back was chafed from the rug each time he plunged into her. She was raw inside and began to bleed. Her almost violent screams of ecstasy overshadowed the tv, eyes welled.

"Don't... stop," she muttered when Jeremy noticed the blood on the carpet.

He thrust harder and more furiously. Then it was over.

"I love you, baby," he said.

"I know," she said, stroking his cheek contentedly.

Natalie was worn, battered, hurting on the outside but felt satiated, whole with Jeremy.

"I love you," she said.

They slept holding each other.

When morning came, Natalie peeled herself out from Jeremy's arms as he lay sleeping, made herself as presentable as possible given the night she had, and crept out quietly. She took a cab home to get herself together for work. When she arrived at her apartment, Natalie caught a glimpse of herself in the vestibule mirror. She had a black eye, cuts on her lips, deep teeth marks on her neck. She could feel the fire of rug burns on her back. Natalie felt it was all worth it to have seen Jeremy again. She loved him, needed him.

Chapter Nine

Natalie arrived at work wearing a sleeveless turtleneck and layers of foundation to hide her love wounds. When Peter walked in, she stopped by his office.

"Good news," she said. "JRMD agreed to Enrique's price. We're done here. 'Book 'em, Danno' as they say."

"That's my girl. God, you look awful. What the hell happened to you?"

"All in a day's work," she replied, turned abruptly and left his office.

When Natalie returned to her desk, her message light was blinking. "Natalie. Enrique here. Call me."

She returned his call immediately on his private line. "Enrique, what's up?"

"Natalie, I've called to tell you my electronics division is no longer for sale."

Her stomach sank. "What happened to make you change your mind?"

"I got a call from Jeremy Dalton a little while ago."

Her heart started to beat fast.

"You remember... from my party. Well, he told me he was the buyer and that he agreed to my price but... he added some conditions that I'm not comfortable with. I don't want to get into the irritating details but he and I have done business in the past and have some tainted history. Essentially, he would be asking me to screw my son as he steps into his new position. My grandfather founded this company out of the shirt off his back, passed it to my father, and he to me. The money JRMD is willing to put up is not worth my son's future, or destroying my relationship with your firm by embroiling you and Peter in one of Jeremy's underhanded deals. I'm sorry. I'm going to give Peter a call and just tell him we've changed our minds due to market conditions but I wanted to talk to you personally because one of Jeremy's 'conditions' would have left you... Well, it doesn't really matter. It's over, in any case, and that's all that really needs to be said."

Natalie was numb when she hung up the phone. She didn't understand what had happened. She sat staring at her phone console in a trance. Minutes later she was startled out of her dream state when Peter arrived at her desk.

"I just got a call from Enrique," he said. "The deal's off. Timing's not right. He said something about picking up discussions again in six months or a year after 'sonny boy's' been in charge, if the market volatility dies down. My wife already had the 'commish' spent on redoing our living room and a trip to Cayman. The big guys in the corner are gonna love this. Whatever. Just wanted to let you know. Oh, he also said... he was concerned about you. That I should watch out for you. Don't know what the hell that means. I'm really not good with the touchy feely stuff. Hey, Nash,..." He walked away to catch a word with Nashiro on a new deal.

Natalie's phone rang. It was Jeremy.

"You left me... again," he said in a sinister voice.

"I had to get ready for work," she said distracted by his tone. "I didn't have my stuff with me or a change of clothes. You were sleeping so peacefully." She did not want to displease him. Her stomach was tumble-saulting. "I didn't want to wake you... What happened with Santiago? He called just a little while ago saying..."

"I've given you my love once more and you've rejected me, again... This... is not... a game. But you're too caught up in your world to see... Three strikes... and you're out, I'm afraid." Jeremy blurted and the line went dead.

Natalie was shaken. Everything seemed to be happening so quickly she didn't have time enough to make sense of Enrique's call or now Jeremy's. She wanted to know what he had said to Santiago about her that concerned him enough to mention something to her boss. At the very least, she wanted to know that much. Natalie had no way to contact him. Quickly she pressed the return call button on her phone that dials back the telephone number of the last call received. It rang and rang. No one answered. The digital display listed the number. She jotted it down and called the operator.

"I just received a called from... Can you tell me where that is?"

"Let me check. Yes that's a pay phone in lower Manhattan at 865 Water Street."

"Thanks." Natalie hurried to slam the phone down and raced to the elevator. That was her company's address. Jeremy was calling from the lobby. By the time she got downstairs, all the pay phones were vacant. She looked around the black marble lounge area, through the glass windows, and outside the entrance. He was gone. Natalie returned to her office and shut the door. She called the Royale.

"Jeremy Dalton, please."

"He checked out this morning," the clerk said.

Natalie remembered seeing Cal Reynolds' phone number in Peter's file she still had from the day before. She dialed his number and got a recording. The number had been disconnected. Natalie went on the internet and looked for listings for Jeremy Dalton, JRMD, and Cal Reynolds. Nothing. Jeremy had disappeared again.

Several days passed. Natalie thought Jeremy might call but he did not. She was perturbed by everything that had happened and wanted to know more about who he was. Natalie hired a private detective to find him. A friend of hers from graduate school had married a private investigator that had his own firm.

"Mark, hi. It's Natalie Baylor. Katie's friend from Stern."

"How's it going?"

"Pretty good."

"Are you still in the people finding business?"

"Yes, if you want to call it that."

"Well, I need some help in locating someone. Actually it's really not even locating but really finding out about someone. He's a business associate who disappears mysteriously—a lot. I want to know who he is and what his story is. He doesn't seem to be a trustworthy guy and I need more information on him that he isn't willing to reveal. Do you think you can help?"

"I can try. Why don't you tell me what you know about him and I'll see what I can dig up. I'll call you when I have something concrete."

Natalie gave him the little information she did have—what was on his business card that was of no use anymore, his business associate's defunct telephone number, how and where they met up each time, a physical description, and a $5,000 cash retainer.

After three weeks, Mark called her at home around eight in the evening. She had just walked in from work when she heard the phone ring.

"Natalie. It's Mark. I have some not so good news. This guy of yours is invisible. There is nothing to speak of in terms of a path that he leaves behind when he moves on, which leads me to believe he has some type of criminal past from a long time ago and has to keep himself underground. He surfaces every now and then, but I'm sure he is using aliases and that he has a pretty big wad of cash supporting his underground life. He's got to be paying people off to keep quiet about knowing him or intimidating them to help them keep their mouths shut. What I was able to find out was that there are no credit reports on him or charge cards in his name, no bank accounts and, in the few places I could confirm that he had been, he paid for everything in cash. You said he invests in real estate and art. There was nothing there either. No property is listed in his name here or abroad. No auction house, large or small, has ever heard of him or admits to knowing him when I showed anyone the rendering we did. In other words, I have nothing to tell you but to be very careful, particularly about getting together with him. He is very smart and knows how to cover his tracks impeccably. I wish I had more to tell you. There's really nothing else I can do. I'm sorry."

"I appreciate all the time you invested in this. I know you do thorough work. Katie probably shared more than she should have with me over the years. That's why I called you."

Natalie sat on her couch dazed, numb. She did not expect this. Natalie thought Mark would find something. She grabbed Chuckles and the unopened pint of Alpine Cliff's banana with chocolate sprinkles ice cream from her freezer. She ate spoonful after spoonful trying to comfort herself, clutching her soft friend with tears in her eyes. Who was this man she thought she loved, who she had given herself to? Natalie felt violated—emotionally raped. Could she trust her judgment, her heart? She didn't know. All she was certain of was that her wedding was ten days away and Natalie dreaded thinking of it and David.

In her sugar stupor, she reached for her phone to call her sister. "A, it's me. Sorry to call so late. Hope I didn't wake the kids."

"It's your usual thoughtful self. What is it?"

"I know you and Mom have been working hard on a shower for me for Saturday afternoon. I'm not gonna be able to make it. I've got some things I need to do for work before I head out for three weeks. Just put it on my tab."

"You are such a selfish bitch. This is not just about you. You'd think the world fuckin' revolves around your scrawny ass…"

Natalie depressed the receiver and disconnected her sister mid insult. She could not face her family and friends playing the part of the glowing bride-to-be. The thought made her sick. She was mourning the loss of the only person who she felt loved by. Natalie wished she could go back in time to the night she and Jeremy pledged themselves to each other to tell him she would stay cocooned in his arms forever, not returning to her life. It didn't matter what his real name was or if he was someone with a dark past. He loved her. But nothing could change that now. Jeremy was gone—without a trace.

Chapter Ten

Natalie's father called her Friday afternoon at the office. During a lull in the market, she made the mistake of answering her phone.

"Adrian called this morning," her father said in a gruff voice. "She said you backed out of going to your own shower tomorrow. You better not pull any of that crap next weekend. The whole firm'll be there Sunday morning at 10 AM and you will be there. You don't want to be treated like a little girl anymore, so stop acting like one. You have obligations, commitments. I don't have time to be bothered with this kind of stuff. Just be there. Do you understand?"

"No," she said defiantly. "Maybe I should put you on speaker and you can scream it across the whole God damn trading floor. Perhaps that'll make your super-sized ego happy. It's always a pleasure to hear from you, Daddy. And it's good to know my happiness is of foremost concern to you.

You and David come from the same revolting mold. Maybe you should be the one marrying him."

Natalie disconnected her father. This was the first time she ever stood up to him. When Natalie put the receiver down, her hand lingered thinking she should call him back to apologize. Her phone rang again. It was Gunta wanting to discuss his next hostile takeover victim. The distraction he provided was the only reason Natalie didn't yield to her father.

The following Friday was Natalie's last day at work before her wedding and honeymoon. She notified her clients to work directly with Peter while she was gone and tied up any loose ends on her current deals. Natalie was only working a half-day so that she could pick up and, if necessary, have another final fitting for her Vera Wang gown. She looked drawn. Over the last week, her appetite had been almost completely non-existent except for an occasional dose of her favorite ice cream—her comfort food. Just before she was heading out, around noon, Peter walked into her office.

"Hey, Nat, it's been so crazy I haven't had time to do anything formal to give you a proper send off," Peter said. "If you have time, I can corral the team and we'll go to Corrina's for lunch. I know you love their *penne pomodoro*."

"I appreciate the offer but I don't have the time. I don't think I could eat anyway. We can do it when I get back if you want. It's no biggie. I'll see you at the reception. I finally get to meet the wife you're always whining about. Can't wait. My clients are holding back alot of their business this week just so they can work with you."

Pete's face had a look of panic.

"Joking... Seriously, though, it was a good move you taking my book while I'm gone. They feel all gooey inside that the head guy'll be servicing them so don't screw anything up. Maybe you can make us some money while I'm out. You're just gonna love Gunta. He's so much fun to work with," she said sarcastically. "Gotta go." Natalie rushed to catch an elevator that just opened.

As soon as Natalie was out of sight, Pete's phone rang.

"Weissman, here."

"Peter?"

"Yeah."

"This is Gunta Handelsman. I understand you and I will be working together while your star producer is on holiday. Weissman... where are you from?"

"Jersey."

"From England? Really?"

"No, the New... Jersey."

"Yes, well..."

The rehearsal dinner was held Saturday night at The Tradewinds in the Garden Room. Natalie had asked her mother to cancel the run-through of the ceremony and have everyone meet at the restaurant. David was not aware that Natalie was by his side during their elaborate meal. He did not notice that she was upset, distracted. He was focused on conversing with his best man, Jason Waxley, his biggest client. David had told Natalie that he didn't even like Jason, that the only reason he had asked him to be his best man was to further their business relationship.

Natalie did not touch her food. Neither her sister nor her father acknowledged her. She sat isolated, alone though surrounded by fifty of her friends and relatives in her own private purgatory. She felt that she could burst into tears at any minute. And she did, privately, with her mother in the ladies lounge.

Natalie excused herself from the table. Her mother sensed her daughter was upset and followed her.

"Mother, I don't love him."

"Oh, God, Natalie. I feel like this is my fault. Maybe if I stood up to your father when he concocted this idea about you marrying David and keeping all the money in the family my little girl wouldn't be in tears the night before her wedding. I'm so sorry. You deserve better, to be happy, to be with a man you love…" She stroked Natalie's hair. "David loves you… in his own way, I'm sure."

Natalie sobbed uncontrollably. "David doesn't love me. Neither he nor Daddy know how to love someone."

Her mother took a deep breath. "You can still call it off if that's what you really want."

"I can't do that," she said through a mask of tears. "I'm in too deep. Daddy would... David's the son he's always dreamt of having." She tried to catch her breath.

Underneath the tears and anger, Natalie had hoped that she would have heard from Jeremy, that he would have resurfaced and rescued her from a loveless union. Her tears were more for that reason than any other. She could not share that with her mother.

Natalie's mother wiped away her daughter's tears. "Honey, why don't we get you in a cab. You go home and rest. Maybe tomorrow things will look brighter. I'll go back to the dinner and just say you wanted to get a good night's rest before the big day. It'll be fine. You know we're staying in the corporate apartment tonight. I'm a phone call away if you need to talk." She hugged Natalie, walked with her to the maitre d's desk, and waved to her daughter holding back her own tears as the taxi drove off.

When Natalie got back to her apartment she checked her messages at work and on her cell phone. There was nothing. And her machine at home was dark. No flashing light. She had prayed that Jeremy had called her. Natalie walked over to the window and looked up at the glowing moon hoping Jeremy was thinking of her gazing at the radiance of the same moon. It was all they could now share, she thought.

Natalie crawled under her bed covers fully clothed. She stared off daydreaming about what the last few weeks and the rest of her life could have been like if she had stayed with Jeremy. Natalie felt hollow without his attention. She craved to be held by him again—nourished by his touch, to look into his eyes and feel the depth of his soul, to have him in her—joined as one. Clutching the cross Jeremy had given her, she yearned to feel whole as she had when she was with him. Jeremy had satisfied a deep, emotional hunger in a way that no one else ever had.

Natalie lay in her bed in a self-induced trance, dreading what would happen the next morning. She had to decide whether to cause intolerable anger in her father or abysmal unhappiness for herself. Burning hot bile churned in her stomach. Finally, around 4 AM, her body and mind succumbed to exhaustion. She slept only because her eyes could no longer remain open.

The phone rang shortly after 7 AM. It was Natalie's mother calling out of concern for her daughter.

"Hello," Natalie said in a raspy voice.

"How are you feeling, dear?" her mother asked with trepidation.

"Like hell. But it's all part of the joy… When Jeannette gets there, can you send her over here to do my hair and make-up? I want to be alone. I can't deal with the commotion with everyone meeting up over there. I need to be in a calmer atmosphere."

"I'll take care of it. Do you want me to come with her?"

"No. It's okay. You enjoy all the mother-of-the-bride attention. I don't want to drag you down with me. One of us is bad enough. Believe me. I'll see you at The Inn at quarter to ten."

Natalie reluctantly pulled herself out of bed in her clothes from the day before. The sun was shining brightly, glistening on the reservoir. It was a beautiful day for an outdoor garden wedding. She traipsed into the shower letting the steaming hot water soak her head with her eyes shut. Natalie prayed that when she opened them she would discover this was just another one of her nightmares. But it was not. "This can't be happening," Natalie said to herself. "I have to be dreaming." This moment felt surreal, like she was watching it unfold as if it were someone else's life.

Jeannette arrived at Natalie's at 8:30. "We are going to turn that frown upside down and bedazzle your guests," she said.

"I'm definitely going to need waterproof mascara today," Natalie said despondently.

Jeannette was very helpful in relaxing Natalie. She distracted her with funny anecdotes about her eccentric clientele, helped her dress, and insisted Natalie have a swig of vodka to calm her bridal nerves.

Natalie was exquisite. She looked as though she stepped off the cover of one of the bridal magazines wearing crisp white French silk that gently outlined her slender hips, buttocks, and legs. A tight bodice pressed her breasts up in an Elizabethan manner. Her alabaster neck was adorned with a pearl choker and her chestnut curls were in an upswept do decorated with carefully placed pearl stickpins. Natalie placed the cross necklace Jeremy gave her in her bra pressing against her heart.

Natalie was in an ethereal daze through the garden ceremony held at Inn on the Park in the middle of Central Park. Escorted on her father's arm, three hundred fifty people looked on as she walked, one foot in front of the other, trembling down the aisle. Natalie was so consumed by her own thoughts, she didn't hear the processional music. When she looked at David, unemotional, stoic, Natalie lost her balance as if she were about to faint. Her father pulled her along. Natalie's helpless eyes locked with her mother's who looked as though her heart was breaking. She wanted her mother to grab her and pull her out of the pit of quicksand she was being sucked into. Adrian looked away when Natalie handed her the white rose she was carrying. Natalie wanted to run away forever.

"Please join hands," the reverend said in a billowing voice.

Natalie's stomach became queasy at David's touch. Her face, flush.

The back of her neck, moist. It took all her energy to remain standing for the twenty-minute ceremony. When the reverend instructed David to kiss his bride, Natalie turned her head slightly ensuring his kiss did not land on her lips. The recession up the aisle was the last time she saw David until it was time to leave. The champagne reception was also held in the garden and a formal luncheon was served inside. David spent the afternoon schmoozing with his colleagues, clients, and new father-in-law puffing on cigars and sipping dry martinis. He was nowhere to be found for their first dance to the horror of friends and family. Natalie was relieved.

As the last of the guests filtered out after the reception and overly lengthy feast, Natalie and her mother organized the numerous piles of gifts while David, his father, and Natalie's father traded stories at the bar with deep belly laughs and guffaws.

The sun was dipping low in the sky when Natalie and David were funneled into the waiting limousine outside. They spent the night in the bridal suite overlooking the pond at the Park Grande Hotel on Central Park South. When they first arrived, David gave the bellman twenty dollars to carry Natalie across the threshold so that he could use the phone. His beeper had gone off. She declined the young man's awkward but gracious offer. Natalie changed out of her gown into a white satin slinky nightshirt and removed her make-up. David remained on the telephone for more than an hour. When he was finished, he took his tuxedo jacket and tie off. He tore open Natalie's nightshirt.

"What the hell are you doing?" she exclaimed. "This was expensive and it's brand new."

David didn't respond to her outburst. He unzipped his pants, bent her forward and forced himself on her. He held onto her breasts as if they were reins pounding himself into her abusively without romance, without passion. At his peak of arousal, he pulled out ejaculating all over her nightshirt. Another power trip, not lovemaking. After pleasuring himself, David put himself back in his pants and poured himself a glass of Grand Marnier. Natalie dropped to the floor when he let her go.

"Want anything?" David asked.

Natalie was surprised he asked. She stood up and raced to the bathroom. She threw up uncontrollably. Retching. Gagging.

"What's up?" he asked, poking his head in the doorway.

"Just the festivities, I'm sure," Natalie replied lethargically, wiping her lips with her forearm while leaning over the porcelain toilet bowl.

"Come to bed when you're done," David said with an icy air and closed the door behind him.

Natalie whisked off her torn, sperm-covered nightshirt and tossed it in the decorative garbage bin under the sink. She lay on the cool tile floor naked, alone. After she thought David expired from his twelve-hour marathon consumption of alcohol, she crept out of the bathroom and slept on the ottoman while he laid diagonally across the king size bed. She was sick.

The next morning, by the time David awoke from his stupor around 9 AM, Natalie was dressed and packed. They had to be at the airport by noon to leave for their honeymoon.

"I forgot my purse last night when we left," she said while he tried to focus. "The banquet manager gave it to my mother. I'm going to run over to their apartment and pick it up."

"Whatever. Just make sure you don't stay there gabbing and make us miss our flight."

Dozens of pigeons were gathered on the promenade outside the hotel basking in the sun. Natalie walked a few short blocks up Fifth Avenue.

"Congratulations, Ms. Baylor" the doorman said. "Or should I say Mrs. Hughes?"

Natalie didn't respond to his question. "Did my father leave yet?" she asked.

"Yes ma'am. Bright and early."

"Thanks."

Natalie and her mother shared a pot of herbal tea and bagels from

Zabar's in the living room twenty-five stories up overlooking the park. They compared fashion notes on what the wedding guests had worn and the conversations they overheard.

"One of Adrian's friends had a Polaroid camera and snapped a few shots during the ceremony," her mother said. "She left them with me last night if you're interested in seeing them." She took them out of her purse.

Natalie casually thumbed through the first three photos. But on the last one she sat staring at it intently with a perplexed scowl. She became agitated, nervous. Jeremy was in the photograph—standing in the back of the garden at The Inn watching the ceremony with an angry look.

"I've got to go, Mother."

"What is it, dear?" her mother asked with concern.

"I've just got to go."

Natalie ran back to the hotel dodging cars on Central Park South. She had a terrified, quivering feeling in her stomach. When she arrived back at their room, the door was slightly open. Natalie started to shake. She pushed the door open with her foot. "David?" she called. There was no answer. She walked into the entranceway. "Holy fucking shit!" she cried out.

David was strung up by his neck, naked, hanging from the crystal chandelier with a rusted red-handled switchblade jabbed into his chest. Blood was dripping from his feet onto the white carpet. His hands were tied together behind his back. Dangling from his fingers was the gold chain and cross that Natalie had given to Jeremy.

Natalie had a sudden shooting pain in her head. She started to hyperventilate and thought she was having a heart attack. "Oh, my God," she said over and over again. Natalie turned in circles looking for Jeremy and a trace of evidence that he was still there. She knew he had done this. But he was gone. Natalie grabbed a washcloth from the bathroom and picked up the telephone receiver with it and dialed 911.

At first when she tried to speak only air came out.

"Hello. Is anyone there?" the operator asked repeatedly.

"My husband... has been... stabbed," she blurted out between ragged breaths.

David was dead.

Chapter Eleven

When the police arrived, Natalie was pacing in the hallway by the elevator. Her nerves were shaken thinking that her need, her hunger for love was the cause of David's death. She loathed him for not loving her the way she craved to be loved. He lacked the capacity to care for her, for any real emotion but she never wished that he be tortured, bludgeoned, killed. Natalie's abysmal thirst to be desired had become a crime. If David had been more nurturing, Jeremy would not have been able to entice her. Her spirit, weakened from a lifetime of failed attempts to gain her father's love and approval, rendered her easy prey and now... David... dead.

"I'm Lieutenant Grealy," an older gentleman with salt and pepper hair said. "Where's the victim?"

Natalie couldn't speak. Trembling, she pointed into their suite looking away.

Light bulbs flashed for several minutes inside. Investigators took their time dusting for fingerprints, collecting bloodstain samples, and questioning hotel personnel.

"I'm Detective Johnson," a young, stout black woman dressed in a blue uniform said. "I'd like to ask you a few questions about what happened."

Natalie nodded.

"…Let me see if I have this right," the officer said. "You were married yesterday? You left for an hour or so this morning? You came back and found your husband like this?…"

After forty-five minutes of interrogation, Natalie looked down at her watch realizing their flight to Tahiti had left five minutes ago. She felt the police immediately thought she killed David. And they did… until they discovered that David had ordered room service several minutes after Natalie was seen on the hotel lobby camera leaving and the police confirmed the call to in-room dining had been placed from their room. Someone else had killed David but the police thought Natalie arranged to have it done. Natalie called her mother on her cell phone.

"Mother, I'm at the hotel. I need you to come over right away… and bring Daddy. I think I'm going to need his help."

When her parents arrived, her father took the lieutenant aside to speak with him privately.

David's death was on the front page of the newspaper the next morning. "Groom Murdered in Park Grande Bridal Suite." The sub-heading read "Victim Partner at Prestigious Law Firm of Baylor, Sussman, Langford, and Hughes."

A prayer service was held in David's honor by his parents at a chapel on Amsterdam Avenue Tuesday morning. His body was being held by the police for further investigation.

"How could you let this happen?" Natalie's father screamed at her when she arrived. He was shaking yesterday's paper that bore that headline at her.

She kept her sunglasses on and walked past him in silence to take a seat by her mother who was sitting quietly, praying. Natalie's mother held her hand. The same guests that were at the wedding two days before filtered into the chapel speaking in hushed whispers. The reverend that married Natalie and David began to speak. Natalie did not hear a word of his eulogy. She did not outwardly grieve over David's death or shed a tear. She was stoic, motionless. Natalie was lost in her own private misery obsessing over the cloud of suspicion she felt hanging over her by the police for David's death. In order to save herself, she was going to have to lead them to Jeremy. This thought was so morose to her, Natalie wished it were she that was being eulogized instead of David.

The next morning Natalie telephoned her mother. She had stayed at her apartment the night before. Her parents had returned to Westchester.

"Mother, I know who did it."

"What do you mean?"

"I know who killed David."

"How would you know that?" she asked with a startled tone.

"..,.I had... You know... There was someone else... when I was in France..."

Her mother did not say anything.

"I had given him the cross necklace you gave me when... after I was... so that I wouldn't be alone... that God would always be watching out for me. It was hanging from David's hand when I found him." Natalie said as she began to sob. "Mother, he was there... at the wedding... in one of the photos you showed me. That's why I got so upset and left like I did. I had a really bad feeling..."

"Oh, my God, Natalie. If you're certain, you've got to tell the police otherwise... I don't know if you're father's 'friends' can help get you out of this... You have no choice."

"I know," Natalie said, wiping her tears.

"You need to talk to the police right away. Who knows what else he may do. I'll go with you. I'll meet you at your apartment in an hour."

"John, would you let my daughter know I'm here and I'll wait downstairs for her," Natalie's mother said to the doorman when she arrived.

He rang Natalie on the intercom while her mother stepped off the sidewalk and tried to hail a cab.

Natalie came downstairs minutes later. Suddenly, she heard the doorman scream.

"Mrs. Baylor." Almost knocking Natalie over as she came through the doorway, John grabbed Natalie's mother, pulling her back from the street. A black Jaguar with smoked windows frantically racing down Central Park West, tires screeching, came within inches of hitting Natalie's mother, swerving with deliberate intent, aiming for her. Natalie watched the car drive off in horror. Her mother and the doorman were lying on the ground scraped and cut from falling abruptly onto the concrete.

"Are you okay?" Natalie shrieked. "You could have been killed." She helped them to stand up and held onto her mother's arm so she could regain her balance.

"Do you want me to call the police?" John asked.

"We were heading over to the precinct," Natalie's mother said.

"Are you okay, John?" Natalie asked.

"I'm fine. I'm just glad I saw him coming."

"Thank you," Natalie said with a heartfelt tone, taking John's hand.

"Mother, this was not an accident," Natalie said when they were safely in a taxi. "My phone must be tapped. I'm sure that was him."

"Natalie, I knew when you called me before you came home from your trip that there had been someone. But what kind of person is this—that you could have feelings for him—who does these kinds of things?"

"There is so much I don't know or understand... I really loved him." Her eyes began to well as she looked away staring out the window. "I've never felt that way for anyone before or thought anyone loved me like he did. If I had just stayed with him... none of this would have happened. I came home to break it off with David face to face and try and network myself into a job over there. But he didn't believe me."

The cab arrived at the police station.

"Is Lieutenant Grealy here?" Natalie asked the young lady behind the glass window in the reception area.

The officer with the salt and pepper hair greeted them.

"What can I do for you ladies?" he asked, distracted and agitated.

Natalie and her mother met with him for less than five minutes telling him that they knew who killed David and that it was Jeremy.

"We'll look into that. Thanks for coming down," he said, shuffling them out.

As they were leaving, the black female officer that had questioned Natalie the day David was killed approached them. "You're the young lady whose husband was killed at the hotel the day after you all got married.

Detective Johnson. I couldn't help but overhear you with the lieutenant. He's only gonna pass on that name you gave him to me to look into. If you have a few minutes, maybe I can ask you a few questions and track this guy down."

The detective escorted them into a room with gray walls, no windows, and a rickety wooden table and chairs. "Let me guess, you had an affair and this Jeremy guy was your lover."

Natalie was uncomfortable with the blunt accusatory tone of the officer but answered her. "Yes."

"How do you know it's him?"

Natalie told her about the necklace hanging from David's hand. She also told the officer that she believed he just attempted to kill her mother and that her phone may have a wire on it.

"I'm gonna need you to tell me everything you know about this guy," the officer said.

And Natalie did. Every morsel she shared felt like she was losing a piece of herself.

"We'll run a profile on him and we'll test your phone, see if it has a wire on it. I'll let you know. If anything else happens, here's my card. Call me."

"Thank you for going with me, Mother," Natalie said embracing her outside the station.

"Do you want me to stay with you?" her mother asked.

"I'll be okay. You go on home. If dinner isn't on the table when 'you know who' comes barreling through the door, there'll be hell to pay. I better let you go."

Natalie left her mother on the street. They went their separate ways. Natalie walked home, trudging aimlessly. The police precinct was only ten blocks from her apartment, but it took her nearly an hour to wind her way through the fog she was in mentally to make it home. Though Natalie didn't love David, she did not wish any harm to come to him. She imagined what a horrific end he had. Was he stabbed and then hung or hung, then stabbed? Did he gasp for air or did he go quickly? Did he know who Jeremy was to her? Would he have cared? Her mind festered with puzzles that would remain unsolved.

Still, Natalie's heart ached with a deep pain from Jeremy's disappearance, the excruciating loss of his love, a rejection beyond anything she could heal from. And then to have killed David, in Natalie's mind, was an act of anger, jealousy, but also love. If he didn't love her, she thought, he would not have done this. Natalie felt comforted by understanding that, in a twisted way, he still cared for her. Jeremy was a part of her life. He was not gone. He knew where she was getting married, what hotel she and David would be at, that she and her mother would be outside her building at a certain time. Jeremy was with her.

When Natalie returned home, she walked over to her phone, melancholy, and caressed her headset before putting it on. She dialed her cell phone number and got her own voice mail.

"I know you can hear me and that you are watching me," she said slowly. "Why did you leave me? You didn't have to go away. I meant what I said. I was going to return to you. But I had to do it in my own way. When you disappeared I felt I had no choice but to marry David. I prayed up until the moment I said those vows that you would return. You didn't have to kill him." She started to cry. "I told you... I didn't love him. My father... pushed me into marrying him. Now everything... is a nightmare." Natalie was sobbing. "The worst part... is that... we can never be together." She could not stop her tears. "I've... got to go," she said, sniffling and disconnected the call.

Natalie walked into the bathroom to get some tissues to wipe her tears. "Aaaahhhh!" she screamed in horror when she turned the bathroom light on. 'You betrayed me, Angel,' was written in blood on a cracked, broken vanity mirror. The sink was covered with blood. Her white islet towels were blood-soaked. And the antique atomizer her grandmother had given her was gone, filled with her favorite perfume, Contessa, the one she wore everyday, the scent Jeremy loved to inhale. She was shaking. She ran down ten flights of stairs to the doorman.

141

"John, did you see anyone go up to my apartment while I was out with my mother," she asked, panting and out of breath.

"No one, Ms. Baylor. Is everything okay?"

Natalie could not speak or catch her breath. She shook her head no. "Can I... use your phone, John?" she blurted out. "I have to... call the police."

The doorman pulled the phone out from under the desk.

Natalie dialed the operator and asked for the number for the four-teenth precinct.

"Detective... Johnson, please."

"Johnson. Homicide."

"It's Natalie Baylor. He was... in my... apartment. When I got back..."

Natalie told the police officer what had happened.

"I'll send someone over," she said.

Detective Johnson called around seven-o'clock that evening. "The police analyzed the blood in your bathroom," she said. "The report stated it matched David's. That's all I know. They had no other information."

Natalie was afraid, and comforted, to be in her apartment that night. She felt scared that Jeremy might harm her but she wanted to feel his presence somehow. Her mother told her to stay in Westchester with her but

Natalie thought Jeremy would be anywhere she went and did not want to endanger anyone but herself. She toured through her apartment as if she were at a museum wondering what he may have touched or been near earlier that day. She imagined him trying to figure out what things were important to her, like the perfume. Natalie knew he had to have touched the front door when he entered. She grabbed Chuckles and tightly hugged him as she rested her back against the door. She slid down to sit on the floor and then reached up touching the handle imagining Jeremy's hand caressing her hand, her eyes closed.

The ringing of the phone startled Natalie. She let the answering machine pick up the call.

"Is this the way you love someone?" It was Jeremy.

Natalie quickly crawled to her coffee table where the answering machine sat. She placed her hand on it. She wanted to pick up the receiver but her arms felt suddenly paralyzed. Did the police have a tap on her phone?

"I know you're there... and you won't pick up the phone to talk to me... You've made me very angry again... going to the police. The only crime I am guilty of is loving you, Princess." The line went dead.

"Don't go," Natalie screamed with her hands cupping her closed eyes. She placed her head on the answering machine, her ear to the speaker. "Don't... go," she said trailing off. "Just stay with me... I don't want to be alone."

Jeremy was gone. He slipped through her fingers.

He left Natalie with recurring images of her rape... 'Princess... Princess... Princess...' The word reverberated in her mind. 'We can do this the easy way, Princess, or the hard way?' 'You don't even know who I am. Do you Princess?' 'Was it everything you thought it would be, Princess?'... Thwack.

Natalie held her head. She thought it was going to explode. "Stooooop!" she screamed. She cried. Black mascara ran down her cheeks. Natalie got up from the floor, legs wobbling, with Chuckles and laid down on her bed, catatonic, trying to recuperate from her nightmare like an epileptic after a fit. She kept all the lights on in her apartment. She was afraid to be in the dark, alone. She just wanted Jeremy to hold her once more. Then everything would be all right.

Around midnight, the phone rang. Natalie jumped from her stupor, her heart beating fast. It was completely dark outside. All the lights were still on in her apartment.

"Hello," Natalie said clearing her throat.

No one answered.

"Hello," she said again. "...Why are you doing this to me?"

There was no reply. Only the rhythm of what Natalie sensed was Jeremy's breath.

"Stay with me… Don't leave me…" Natalie pleaded. She clutched the phone pressing it to her ear with one hand while her other held the cross tightly. Natalie drifted off peacefully feeling Jeremy was near. Around 3 AM, Natalie woke from her slumber from what she thought was the smell of Jeremy's cologne. Natalie imagined she saw him standing in front of her as she lay in bed. She reached out to him, but no one was there. Natalie needed to be loved by Jeremy so deeply that her mind seemed to be playing tricks on her. Alone, she fell into a desolate stupor.

Chapter Twelve

When the next morning came, the loud, incessant beep of the phone lying against Natalie's ear woke her from a sound sleep. Her eyes shot open. The call she believed to be with Jeremy was disconnected. She sat bolt upright in her bed and reached for the cross around her neck. She kept feeling for it but it was not there. She jumped out of bed, tore the bed covers off frantically. The necklace was gone. Natalie's heart beat hard and fast. She could feel her blood pumping through her body. Thinking maybe she took it off before going to sleep, Natalie opened her jewelry box. The chimes rang. Tears welled in her eyes. In her mind, she was in the ice cream parlor and then the woods, being penetrated, bleeding. Thwack. The sound of the tree branch that battered her reverberated in her head. Natalie could almost see the young man's face that was over her and then the image became cloudy and faded. The cross was not there. Natalie slammed the jewelry box closed. She held her throbbing head. Natalie stumbled out of her bedroom into the living room. The front door was open slightly. A single red rose was placed on the coffee table. It had not been there yesterday. Natalie heard a knock on the door. Her entire body shuttered with fear. She gasped. Trembled uncontrollably.

"Ms. Baylor?" It was a woman's voice. The door opened slowly.

Natalie stood frozen, panicked. The door squeaked open.

"Detective Johnson, it's you." Natalie exhaled in relief.

"Your door was open. Is everything all right?" the officer asked.

"I don't know," Natalie said distracted and confused.

"We did find a tap on your phone late yesterday. And now we put one of our own on. The line was open all night. I wanted to see what was going on here. Did this Jeremy guy contact you?"

"...I think so... yes." Natalie hesitated. She couldn't stop trembling.

"Has something else happened?"

Natalie dropped to her knees, sat back on her heals and stared down at the floor.

The detective crouched down on one knee to be at eye level with Natalie. "...We did a search on him, Natalie, with the information you gave me the other day and we can't find Jeremy. The only way I can help you is if you tell me what you know."

Tears ran down Natalie's face. "...He was here... last night... this morning. I don't know exactly. The necklace he gave me... I went to sleep wearing it... and now it's gone... This rose... I think he left it here... The door was open... when you got here..."

"Did you see him?" Detective Johnson asked.

"No," Natalie replied.

"Did you hear anything?"

"He called last night... Didn't you pick that up on your..." Natalie wiped her face.

"The wire went on after midnight. We only detected that your line was open, off the hook. Natalie, are you protecting this guy? If he knows you're talking to the police, you could be in a lot of danger. The only way we can protect you is if you tell us what you know."

"I've told you everything because I tried to find him myself. I hired a private investigator to find him and he couldn't. I told him just what I told you."

"Did this PI come up with anything?"

"All he said was that he was probably someone with a criminal past and was very good at hiding himself because, I guess, that was what he needed to do to survive." With every word she uttered, Natalie felt she was betraying Jeremy.

"This is killing my knee. Why don't we get you up, maybe try

149

sitting in a chair." The officer stood up and extended her hand to Natalie. They sat in the two oversized golden beige club chairs.

"Natalie, I don't think you had anything directly to do with killing your husband. The other officers on the case, they think you killed David but they can't put you at the scene... And the Chief's trying to find something that makes this have an easy solution. He's not digging very deep. He just wants the whole thing to go away. Translation—he wants me to pin Jeremy. I think you're still in love with this mystery man. That's probably why you tried to locate him. You're gonna lead us to him in your own time."

Natalie winced.

"So until that happens, would you mind if I give this PI a call and compare notes. Maybe he uncovered something that clicks with what we have so far which ain't much. It could help. Probably not. But it can't hurt. It's a safer bet if we get to him before he gets to you. Trust me."

Natalie gave the officer Mark's telephone number and walked her to the door locking it behind her. Natalie's stomach swelled with nausea at the thought of leading the police to Jeremy, betraying his love again and again. She wanted to hold him in her private memory bank—a sanctuary where only she could go to be with him. Her emotional heart was shredding at the same time Natalie's intestines were about to erupt. She ran to the bathroom and unloaded the remnants of food from her stomach. Projectile vomit spewed from her contracting gut. She coughed, choked.

Beads of sweat collected on her milk-white forehead. She was steeped in physical and mental agony. Natalie wanted the pain to stop. Everything was contaminating the memory of Jeremy's love.

Later that day, Natalie was feeling a little more composed. She decided to go to Empire Market to pick up some groceries. There was little food in her house. Being so upset, she had not been eating much. Natalie was feeling weak and knew she needed to keep up her physical strength to get through each minute. When she got to the store, Natalie pushed a cart up and down every aisle picking out fresh vegetables and fruit, cereal, soup—all the foods that helped her to feel nurtured and nourished. Her last stop was the frozen section. She went straight to the ice cream. When she found Alpine Cliff's, Natalie searched for her favorite flavor—banana with chocolate sprinkles. There was one carton pushed to the back. Natalie pulled it out. When she looked down at the lid, there was a hand written note—'Meet me in the second car of the uptown A train at five o'clock. Get on at forty-second street. Please do not betray me again by bringing your friends.'

The container fell from Natalie's hands onto the linoleum floor. It blew open and ice cream splattered everywhere. She left her cart full of groceries, ran up and down the aisles searching for Jeremy with the note crumpled in her hand. She looked outside. He was nowhere to be found. Natalie sat on a fire hydrant panting for air outside the store. The automatic entrance doors were opening, closing, opening, closing, while she grasped her chest thinking she was having a heart attack. When her normal breathing pattern returned and the tightness in her chest ceased, Natalie looked down at her wristwatch. It was 4:30.

Without a second thought, Natalie rushed down into the subway at ninety-sixth street to catch a southbound A. Sitting on the rumbling train, she didn't care if her life was in danger. She wanted to see Jeremy again. Calling the police or her 'friends,' as he put it, did not enter her thoughts. Natalie wanted him all to herself, no matter what happened. She exited the train when it stopped at forty-second street and crossed to the front of the uptown platform. The steaming hot station was filled with a throng of silent, lonely, overheated commuters. With trepidation, she waited for the train. It was one minute to five. Natalie heard the wheels and engine of a train entering the station. Her hair blew wildly. Dust flew into her eyes. The train raced by almost knocking her back. It was out of service.

The next train came barreling through and stopped at the station. This time it was the A but the first car was in front of her not the second as the note indicated. Natalie elbowed herself through the crowd to get to the next car. It was packed. She squeezed her way in. Natalie was facing the door when it closed. The train began to move. From behind her, she felt an arm slip around her waist. Natalie was startled, afraid.

"Baby, it's me," Jeremy whispered in her ear softly.

Soothed by his voice, she twisted to face him.

"Don't turn around. This way, if they ask, you can say you didn't see me."

She looked up into the glass of the door at their reflection. Natalie reached her hand up and stroked his smooth face, running her fingers through his soft hair.

"I missed you, baby," he said. "You're every bit as beautiful... The smell of your perfume..." Jeremy inhaled deeply and then kissed Natalie's neck. "I wake up thinking of you. I go to sleep dreaming of you. I love you so much. How could you betray me?"

Natalie turned her head with her eyes closed. She pulled his head closer to hers. "I had no choice..."

"I gave you all of me," he said.

"You were gone... How could you kill him?"

"I wasn't gonna let you be with 'Mr. Wonderful.' He had to go. You're mine, baby. It was the only way."

"Jesus Christ. What's gonna happen to us?"

"They don't have enough to pin this on you. And besides, your dad took care of that lieutenant. He's on coast, almost ready to collect his pension. He's not gonna rock the boat. And... they're not gonna find me... unless... you help them, just like the detective told you today."

Natalie turned her head forward and looked at him in the reflection of the glass. "How did you..."

"Ssshhhh, baby. I'm with you day and night, right by your side," he whispered. "I won't let you be alone..."

"I don't want to be without you," she said, caressing his neck. She felt a chain. It was the one he had given her that was missing.

"I'm sorry I had to take the necklace. It's engraved on the back. I had to get it from you before they got their hands on it..."

Jeremy kissed her.

Natalie wanted to inhale him.

"I want to be with you, forever" he said. "All I ask is that you don't stop loving me. No matter what happens, always remember I love you more than anything in the world. We'll find a way to be together for eternity."

"What should I do?"

"Just lay low. Don't contact that officer anymore. She's too smart. Let some time pass and then I'll get in touch with you. This thing needs to die down—get the heat off." He kissed her.

She wanted to stay with him.

The train stopped.

"You should get out here," Jeremy said, bringing Natalie's hand to his lips and placing a delicate kiss on her fingertips.

She stepped out onto the platform. The doors quickly shut behind her. Natalie looked back. Jeremy was gone, lost in the crowd of isolated strangers on the train as it pulled away. Natalie felt innately loved at her core while she was with him. Satiated. She wanted that sensation to last forever, for no one to destroy or take it away.

Because she had left all her groceries at the store, on her way home, Natalie walked into a Chinese take-out restaurant on Columbus Avenue to get some food to go.

"Vegetable fried rice, hot and sour soup, and broccoli and tofu in garlic sauce, please." Her appetite had returned.

While she was waiting for her food, the six o'clock news was coming on on the tv overhead.

"Our top story tonight... There is still no lead on who killed the groom, David Hughes, partner at the law firm of Baylor, Langford, Sussman and Hughes at the Park Grande Hotel. Police today stated they have followed up on what little information they have gathered but so far there are no named suspects. The investigation continues. We'll keep you updated..."

Natalie paid for her food and left abruptly. She walked home quickly thinking a faster pace would help her leave what she heard on the television behind, but she kept hearing it play over and over in her head. When she arrived home, Natalie sat on the floor of the living room at the coffee table with Chuckles on her lap to comfort her. She didn't want to be alone. Natalie picked up the rose Jeremy had left her, sniffed its fragrant scent, and then stroked her face with it. She placed the rose across from her and dined with it imagining Jeremy was with her. The possibility of reuniting with him eased her anxiety. Knowing he still cared for her, that she was not alone, fed the hungry child that dwelled within her longing heart.

To keep her mind occupied until she and Jeremy could be together, Natalie decided to return to work. Having not been back since David's death, she called Peter on her cell phone and left him a voice mail message after finishing her dinner.

"Hey, Pete. It's Natalie. I wanted to let you know I'm gonna come back to work tomorrow. I think I would be better off keeping busy and being productive for the firm. It's a win-win. Anyway, I'll see you then."

She fell asleep that night dreaming of Jeremy.

Natalie got to work at 7 AM the next morning wearing a simple black jersey dress. She wanted to be there early to go through her mail and messages so that she was as prepared as she could be work-wise. Natalie thought there would be personal reactions to reckon with since David's death had been in the paper and on the news. She knew she would not be able to hide. Natalie's colleagues avoided her as they trickled in one-by-one. No one welcomed her back or expressed condolences. When Peter arrived, as he exited the elevator and walked through the glass doors, he headed straight for her—jacket on, briefcase in hand.

"Hey, Nat. What cha doing here? We didn't expect you…"

"I left you a message but I guess you didn't get it."

"You don't have to do this. If it's too soon you know. Take the time you need… And then call Gunta this morning and let him know you're back. Is he like a descendant from the Third Reich or what?"

"I knew you would get along great," she said sarcastically. "He brings us a ton of business. Sometimes we have to deal with 'unsavory' types to get what we want."

"Brilliant and a tight ass, aahh…" he said in a daydream and then caught himself. "…And call Santiago while you're at it. See if you can resurrect that deal. The boys in the corner office and the penthouse were, how shall I say… pissed as all fuckin' hell. You've moved mountains before, sweet cheeks. You got me movin' and it's only eight o'clock. You really do make a beautiful widow."

When Peter walked away, Natalie telephoned Santiago.

"Enrique, it's Natalie."

"I was so sorry to hear what happened," he said. "My deepest sympathies."

"Thanks. I appreciate that… Pete wanted me to touch base with you to see if there was any chance of resurrecting the deal with you and JRMD."

"If there was, I wouldn't be able to do it with Stevens Worth Aikens."

"Are you moving your business to another investment house?"

"No. I wish it was that simple," he said. "I'm not sure it's a good idea for me to get into it but I'm also not sure if it's smart for me to stay silent either. You know I think very highly of you and I would never want anything bad..."

"It sounds like this is something I need to know," Natalie said.

"I think I've said too much. It would just be a conflict of interest for us to pick up our discussions where we left off. Let's just leave it at that."

While she was on the line with Santiago, the message light on her console had lit up.

"I miss you, baby," she heard in a low, sensual voice. It was Jeremy. "I just want to have you all to myself. No one can love you the way I do. I can't wait till we can be together again."

Natalie started to shake. She was in the woods, pinned under a stranger. She played the message again. She was bleeding, helpless.

"I just wanted to have you all to myself, Angel. Now, no one can know you the way I do."

Natalie played the message again and again. She held her head, eyes closed tight. She could see the face of the young man over her, raping her, hurting her. Natalie started to sweat. A bolt of nausea struck her stomach. Her cheeks started to water. She ran to the bathroom, flinging open one of the stall doors. Natalie dropped to her knees gagging, spewing vomit as the stall door squeaked back and forth behind her. She was alone. Heaving sprawled on the icy tile. Tears rained down from her eyes. She cried and wailed uncontrollably. She could not stop retching. Images of her rape and memories of her lovemaking with Jeremy swirled through her mind like tidal waves in tandem with hurling eruptions from her body. Tender, rough. Intimate, violent. Loving, excruciating. Her head was being sucked into an undertow of mismatched emotions. She hung over the porcelain bowl. Exhausted. Sickened. Relieved. It was over. She now knew who Jeremy was—the man who had forever changed her life.

Chapter Thirteen

Natalie splashed cold water on her face and rinsed her mouth, catching her reflection in the mirror of the ladies' lounge in her office. She was repelled by her own image, not able to make sense of her racing thoughts. How could she love someone who had been so vile to her? How could she not have been innately repulsed by him? Why did she still love him? Natalie couldn't stay at work in the unsteady frame of mind she was in. She needed some air and time to face the memories that had come crashing back. Natalie felt violated as if she had been raped yesterday. She had never been able to understand what happened because of the loss of memory, only remembering bits and pieces. But now, she knew Jeremy had raped her.

Natalie walked to Battery Park and sat on a wooden bench looking out at the boats lilting in the harbor, steeped in self-loathing. What kind of heinous person was she to fall in love with the man who stole her innocence? Natalie's emotions were deadened. Her stomach grew hollow. The ringing of her cell phone strapped to her side startled Natalie out of a dazed state.

"Yeah?"

"Baby, I thought you were going to be at the office today," Jeremy said.

Her eyes welled with tears. "Why? Why did you do this to me?" She wept. "Why did you come back?"

Jeremy was silent.

"I know it was you..." She sobbed uncontrollably. "I can see you, hear you, feel you hurting me..."

"I wish I could hold you and take away your pain. I never meant to hurt you. Please don't stop loving me..." His voice trailed off as Natalie took the phone away from her ear and disconnected his call.

The phone rang again and again. She did not answer. Natalie cupped her face trying to hide from joggers and strollers as they leered. She wanted to cast her phone into the river but stopped herself. It was a way for Jeremy to communicate with her without the police knowing. Why did she care? In frustration, she pushed the ringer button off. In silence, Natalie was forced to be alone with herself, her thoughts, her fears. At that moment, alone was the last thing Natalie wanted to be. She wanted to run, to crawl out from under her own skin, to be anyone but herself. There was no escape. Natalie hated Jeremy and she loved him. Nothing was going to change that. Natalie turned the ringer back on. If she heard Jeremy trying to reach her, she felt his love. Without it, there was only pain.

Natalie couldn't return to the office. She wouldn't be able to act like everything was fine. She decided to walk... in the park, and walk along the Hudson River... up through Tribeca, and walk...along Broadway to Columbus Circle and walk... to the pond in Central Park hoping the further she went, the more of her thoughts she could shed. But there was no way out for Natalie. She wouldn't be able to undo what she now knew. Maybe if she told someone, her self-hatred would be lessened. Sitting against a rock, Natalie dialed her mother.

"Mother, I know," Natalie said. "The memories have been getting more vivid. I know who... raped me."

Her mother didn't say a word.

"It was Jeremy. He was the one who did it." She cried.

"How do you..."

"I can see his face, hear his voice... It was him."

"I thought..." Her mother walked over to her perfume tray in her bedroom, lifted it up with the phone cradled in her neck taking a folded, tattered piece of paper out from underneath. 'Robert McDonough' was scratched in pink crayon. "Natalie, are you certain?"

"Yes," she blurted out through tears.

"Oh, God, Natalie. Are you okay?"

"I don't know how to answer that, Mother. I just don't know… I needed to tell someone. I didn't know what else to do. I hurt so deep inside I can't even imagine being free from this…"

"I am so, so sorry," her mother said from the bottom of her soul.

"I'm gonna go, Mother. I can't talk anymore right now."

When she hung up, Natalie's mother telephoned Detective Johnson.

"Homicide. Johnson."

"This is Natalie Baylor's mother. We met…"

"Yes, Mrs. Baylor. What can I do for you?"

"The man… that killed… my son-in-law… he's the same man… that raped… Natalie."

"What do you mean, raped her?" the officer asked with alarm. "When was your daughter raped, Mrs. Baylor?"

"When she was fifteen. She was hurt very badly and lost most of the memory of what had happened to her but…"

"How do you know it's the same guy?" Detective Johnson asked.

"Please don't… I know," she said, wanting to protect her daughter.

"Were charges ever brought against him?"

"No. My husband would not… Natalie's girl friend who was with her the day it happened knew him and gave me his name just in case I ever needed… It's Robert McDonough," she said, looking down at the piece of paper that Megan had scribbled on years earlier. Her hand was trembling.

"So what you're saying is that Jeremy and Robert are the same guy?" the detective asked.

"Yes. I think so," Natalie's mother answered.

"Mrs. Baylor, do you know if there was a rape kit done at the time?" the officer asked intently.

"Yes, there was but..."

"Let me get to work on this."

When Natalie's father came home that evening, her mother unleashed her anger in a tirade yelling and screeching at him in their vaulted living room. "David's killer is the same guy who raped Natalie, Harv," she said emphatically.

"What the hell are you talking about?" Harv demanded.

"It's true," Betsy insisted.

"It's true," he challenged. "And what reliable source..."

"She remembers. She... remembers," Natalie's mother said with venom.

"She remembers. What does that have to do with what happened to David?" he asked.

"He's been going by a different name probably just to get close to her. I blame you for this, Harv. It's all your fault. If you had let them prosecute him then, we wouldn't be in this mess. David wouldn't be dead. And our daughter's life wouldn't be in jeopardy. You're a selfish, egotistical bastard. All you've ever cared about is your beloved practice, sucking up to your precious clients, money and more money. You wanted to protect your firm's reputation more than your own daughter. Isn't it ironic, Harv, how your firm ended up plastered all over the media anyway? What do the kids today call that? Karmic debt, I believe. Had you just let us do the right thing back then, none of this would have happened. Our daughter is suffering at the hands of this man—again. And he very well may succeed in taking her life this time. Maybe that's what you want. Since she didn't turn out to be the son you wanted, you've spent her entire life blaming her for that."

"The fuck I did. And by the way, that firm kept you under this roof, in this neighborhood, wearing those clothes, took you all over the world… I didn't hear you complaining or see you trying to earn a dime. So don't give me that crap."

"I was perfectly content to raise two daughters. I never asked for any of that and certainly not in place of protecting our child. I hate myself for listening to you, not letting her talk to the police back then, that I let us do this to her. She has never been the same since. She completely lost her sense of who she was. Her innocence was destroyed that day. If it wasn't enough that she was brutally raped and nearly killed, in some sick and warped way, you condemned her for it. God, not to mention forcing her into a marriage she didn't want to better position your damn firm. She went through with it anyway to please you. You thought you were insulating her somehow with your unrealistic expectations and never-ending criticism. She ran to business school to get away from you, your cruelty. And now it enrages you that she doesn't need your money. That's all you would be good for to her. But she's made it on her own."

"Like hell she has. I called my friends on the school's Board and asked them to do me a favor. I'm always asking for favors for her. You think she would have gotten into an ivy league school on her own? That's a laugh."

"Don't you dare take that away from her. It just tears you up that she doesn't need you. If you had just loved her, Harv…"

He stormed out of the living room, into the den slamming the double doors behind him.

Natalie had continued walking and finally made her way back to her apartment. There were a dozen red roses in a golden vase on the night stand by her bed with a card. She staggered toward them.

'I'm so sorry. Please don't stop loving me. I never stopped loving you. You're the best thing that ever happened to me. I've waited a lifetime to be good enough for you,' the card read.

In a fit of anger, Natalie picked up the vase and hurled it against the wall with all her strength. A loud bellowing grunt echoed from the bowels of her spirit as it sailed across the room. The beautiful gold urn was shattered. Water splattered on the wall and soaked her Persian rug. The aromatic flowers were strewn in disarray. Natalie clasped the card to her chest crying, wailing. She rushed over to the flooded remains of the vase trying to piece it together. It was without hope. As Natalie gathered the remnants of glass in her hands, they cut her fingers and began to bleed. "Aaahhh," Natalie screamed. She wrapped her hands with toilet paper to soak up the blood and left the rest of the glass in the puddle despising herself for destroying Jeremy's gift. Natalie picked up each rose, inhaling its scent, and placed them carefully on her bed. She spent a restless night under rose-covered bedding wondering how he had gotten into her apartment again. Was he watching her? Blanketed by Jeremy's love, the flowers—the air of his presence—helped to soothe her.

The next morning, Natalie decided to return to work again trying to keep her mind focused. With bags under her eyes, she removed a black jumpsuit from her closet. She stepped into it and zipped it up the back. It was tight and uncomfortable around her stomach. She changed several times trying to find something that fit more loosely around the middle. Naked, Natalie studied her figure in the full-length, antique wooden mirror that stood in the corner of her bedroom. She looked at her profile, turning from side to side. Her stomach was not the washboard it had been weeks ago. It was slightly rounded, hard. Natalie searched her calendar. She always marked down her cycle. She had not menstruated since the week before she went to France. "God," she cried out gritting her teeth. With the upheaval she and her emotions were experiencing, Natalie had not paid much attention. She thought back to their love making on the beach after Enrique's soiree, the endless love making she and Jeremy shared at his beach home, the night she saw him at his hotel in New York. Natalie had craved for Jeremy to be in her, to surrender her total self to him, for them to be one—no synthetic barrier between them. She did not regret their time together. To feel loved at her core once in her life, Natalie would have risked anything. Everything.

On the way to work, Natalie stopped at Gold's Drug to purchase a home pregnancy kit. When she got to the office, Natalie headed straight to the ladies room, followed the directions on the box. Her face became flush, hot, looking at the results slowly emerging. The test confirmed her fear. She became queasy, lightheaded. The life, now growing within her, she knew, was Jeremy's.

Natalie sat at her desk staring at her stock quote monitor not able to focus.

"What happened yesterday?" Peter asked. "We missed you."

"It was just a little overwhelming. I'm gonna try and stick it out today."

As Peter walked away, a broadcast message popped up on her computer screen.

'I hope you liked the flowers, baby.'

Looking around the trading floor, Natalie wondered how Jeremy could send an internal message. He was everywhere and nowhere. She could not see him, touch him, but he was there. Natalie was scared he was so close, comforted he was near. She wanted to tell him she was carrying his child, to tell him she loved him; to tell him she hated him and stab an emotional knife into his heart hurting him as much as he had hurt her. Natalie couldn't make sense of her polarized feelings. She just tried to concentrate on her work.

Late that afternoon, Natalie's mother received a call from Detective Johnson.

"We were able to pull up a profile on a Robert McDonough, enough to identify him, but there's no criminal history. He's clean. We've tried to locate the rape kit, but it's nowhere to be found so we can't pin the rape on Robert without Natalie's positive identification... Mrs. Baylor, we want to talk to your daughter again and bring in a sketch artist."

Natalie's mother was silent.

"Guys like this don't stop until they get what they want," the detective said. "He will strike again. He clearly has an obsession for your daughter if he came back after all this time. Her life is in danger. Not 'could be' but 'is.' I hope you can convince her to help herself because we can't do this without her."

At home that evening, Natalie was eating her banana and chocolate sprinkles ice cream watching a re-run of "Friends" when the phone rang. It was her mother.

"I told the police, Natalie," she said.

Natalie bolted up in her chair. Her eyes darted around the living room.

"I called that detective and let her know it was the same person who… hurt you, that killed David… They want you to come in to talk to a sketch artist… I had to do it…"

Natalie slammed the phone down. Her breathing was ragged. Her chest was rising and falling rapidly each time she took a breath, exhaled. She knew the police would hear what her mother said through their tap. She knew Jeremy would hear because he was always with her. Panic swept through her body. Natalie paced erratically. Intermittently sitting, holding her head. "God, Mother. How could you be so fucking stupid?" she screamed out. Natalie called her mother back on her cell phone. "Mother, why did you do this to me? I thought you would have known that was in confidence. There is a God damn tap on my line."

"I just wanted to do what was right this time to protect my little girl, the way I didn't before. I'm so sorry, Natalie. I did it to protect you," she said sobbing.

"I think it's a little late... Mother, I know you tried to do the right thing back then. It was Daddy. God forbid he loses a client... He makes me sick... Did you tell the detective that I told you?"

"No."

"Then they can forget it. I'm not going to talk to them again, Mother."

"Don't protect this guy, Natalie. The police say you're in danger."

"I'll take my chances."

"How can you still have feelings for him after knowing...?"

"I can't do this anymore. I have to go..." She was overwhelmed.

When Natalie got to work the next morning, her message light was on.

"You betrayed me, again." It was Jeremy. "You've made me very, very angry, Angel." His tone was biting, vicious. "That was an intimate secret for only you and I to know, for us to share forever. How can I trust you? What do I have to do to have you all to myself?"

The fury in his voice scared her. Natalie knew he heard what her mother said about the police. She had thought they stood another chance to be together. But now, was that over, she thought. He had raped and killed. What if her mother and the police were right? Natalie was more terrified at losing him forever than anything else that Jeremy could do to her.

Over the speaker system, Peter called a meeting mid-morning for his staff. "I need all my directs in the east conference room stat."

Natalie, along with a dozen of her colleagues, filed swiftly into the mahogany-paneled room overlooking the river.

Pete closed the door. "Gonna make this quick... Word came down from the boys in the penthouse, the Feds are pulling our phone tapes, kids. Don't know what they're looking for, so keep it clean out there. This is not the time to be telling your friends about any 'specials' we may be having. Capeesh? Now get back out there. Let's rake in the dinero."

While everyone filtered out, Peter tapped Natalie to stay back. "Hey, Nat, have a sec?"

"Do I want to hear this?" she asked.

"Who's this Johnson dame? Nosing around like you would not believe. Asking a lot of questions about you, your phone log... Did you do that deal with Santiago without Stevens? More importantly, without me? 'Cause if you did, I would have thought you'd give me a piece of that action since I can't get any other kind."

"Tell me you're joking about the Santiago thing."

"Okay. Just thought I'd check. You know... you... me... on our own tropical island, naked."

"Pete, you are one big sexual harassment case waiting to happen. I'm not you're gal. You're just gonna have to continue jacking off fantasizing about me."

"Can you make any suggestions?" he asked playfully.

"Yeah. I'm outta here. I've got work to do."

Although she enjoyed verbal sparring with Peter, Natalie felt her world closing in. When she left the conference room, Natalie went into her office and shut the door. She needed a break from the frenetic activity on the floor—ringing phones, young arrogants shouting orders, bleeping computers.

Minutes later, Sue knocked on the glass. Poked her head in the office. "Hey. Pete said you were back. I didn't see you yesterday. I wanted to say I'm really sorry. I heard about David... I also heard you were a beautiful bride. I have a call for you. There's a Detective Johnson on your top line. Do you want me to tell her you'll call her back?" Sue asked.

Natalie took a deep breath. "I'll take it," she said, picking up the receiver.

"Natalie. Detective Johnson here. Can you talk?"

"Sure," she said with disdain.

"Natalie, you know your mother told me she thinks Jeremy

174

is Robert."

"What do you mean? Who's Robert?"

"Robert McDonough… She said he was the guy who raped you."

Natalie's mind tail-spinned. She was in the ice cream parlor. She was looking at the young man behind the counter. She could see 'Robert McDonough' on the name tag pinned to his white apron. Natalie could hear the chiming of the bells over the door. She was in the woods. He was over her. "We can do this the easy way, Princess, or the hard way." Then suddenly in her mind, she was on the beach. "I, Jeremy Robert, pledge to you, Natalie…" She saw the Santiago Enterprises file on the corner of her desk. She flipped through the notes in the file scribbled in Peter's hand-writing. 'Spoke with JR of JRMD…' 'Met with JR…' JRMD. Jeremy Robert M. Dalton was on the business card he gave her in Paris. Natalie couldn't breath. Her chest heavy. Her head felt as though she had been pelted with bricks. Her face flush. Who was he really?

"Natalie? Are you still there?"

She couldn't speak.

"We know he's been in contact with you at work. Luckily, you securities people record your calls and we've got 'em on tape. We've been monitoring your calls this morning. He left you a message a few minutes ago that we think he's gonna act on." The detective played it for her over the phone.

"You make me so angry, Angel, I could kill you."

"We think you could be in some sort of danger. Don't know if he's gonna act on this or he's just angry. I'm not into taking chances. We're sending over an officer to your apartment tonight. He won't bother you. He'll just stay outside your door. Unless he thinks you're in trouble."

Natalie didn't care if Jeremy did kill her. Her heart and mind were tormented. She couldn't bear another confrontation. Any more questions. Accusations. Threats. She wanted the pain to end.

Chapter Fourteen

Natalie arrived home that evening around 7:30.

Jeremy had been hiding in the stairwell.

When the officer arrived, Jeremy knocked him out with a blow to the back of the head with the barrel of a revolver and then dragged him into the stairway.

"Let me in," Jeremy shouted.

She was afraid. "They're looking for you," she said through the door.

"Open the fucking door."

She let him in. Trembling, scared.

Jeremy was holding the gun at his side. He slammed and locked the door behind him.

"Jeremy. Robert. I don't even know who are you?"

"Jeremy Robert McDonough Dalton. My mother's maiden name was Dalton. My father's name was Robert McDonough. He was rich and successful. I wanted to be someone like him. Not who I was born being. My mother got pregnant at sixteen. Her parents kicked her out. My father beat her and me then left us. Nothing was handed to me. I grew up dirt poor. Not knowing when I was going to eat again. Everyone doesn't have a father to hand them everything like you, Princess. All I was ever certain of was that I loved you."

"If you loved me, then why did you leave me in Cannes?"

"I wanted to test you to see if you would be faithful. You said you needed to go back and take care of things so we could be together. You married someone you said you didn't love. You fucked him on your wedding night," he said, in a fit of rage slamming her with the gun on the side of her face.

She fell to the ground, stunned.

"I saw the remnants of your lovemaking when I went to the hotel. How could you do that? You said you were mine."

Natalie cowered holding her cheek.

Kneeling down, Jeremy took her hand away from her face, grabbed her hair and pressed her head against his, holding her close. His rage suddenly vanished. He kissed her tenderly.

Natalie resisted trying to push him away at first.

He kissed her hard.

She surrendered to his passion pulling him into her. She nestled her head against his chest. "…Why did you do it?" she asked softly staring off.

He held her tight. "I didn't know how else to get close to you. I saw you every day. I was in love with you. You didn't even notice me. You never would have unless I made something of myself. I hated you for not loving me back. You didn't look to see who I was inside. You only noticed guys with rich daddies, big houses, and trust funds like that Danny Mintner. Well, I didn't have any of that."

"I'm sorry for hurting you. I couldn't love someone like Robert. You're right. I never looked at you that way. Even if I had, my father never would have allowed me to be with you. Only guys with a highbrow back-ground. Sons of colleagues who could put money in his bank accounts. I hated David. He sickened me. When he touched me that night, I vomited my guts out when it was over. If you had just come back or called, I would have walked away. I prayed every day you would come back. Something. But there was nothing. I hired an investigator to find you. But you were invisible. I never met anyone like you. Full of passion, love, romance, intellect. Had you just come back, I would have run and never looked back. The only time I ever felt loved by anyone was with you. I loved you. The worst thing I ever experienced was losing you. When you left me in Cannes, I was desperate. I looked for you everywhere. It was as if you never existed at all. Gone... without a trace. The loss I suffered was worse than any death could possibly ever be."

"And now your father is the one suffering the loss and you didn't have to be the one to cause him the pain like if you ran from the altar. I did you a favor... You said you loved me. If you really do love me, come on. Run away with me, Natalie. Right now. I've been waiting my whole life to be with you." He kissed her again, his tongue penetrating her mouth, lips caressing. "We don't have much time," Jeremy said still holding the gun.

From outside the door they heard the static of the policeman's radio. Suddenly, they heard someone banging on the door.

Natalie had a look of panic in her eyes.

"Are you in there, Natalie?" It was Detective Johnson's voice. "Natalie?"

She and another officer slammed themselves into the door forcing it open, and burst into Natalie's apartment.

"Drop your gun," the detective shouted in a stern voice with her pistol drawn.

Jeremy cocked his gun and slowly pointed it at Natalie's head, clutching her close to him with his other arm. "I don't care if they kill me. But I would rather see you dead than spend your life with someone else. What's it gonna be, Natalie?"

She pulled at his forearm trying to free herself from his grip. "Don't!" Natalie screamed with terror. "I'm pregnant... with your child."

Bang!

"Aaahh," Jeremy screamed arching forward. Collapsed. Thunk. Hitting the floor. Detective Johnson had fired a single shot to his chest.

"Nooooo!" Natalie shrieked. She cradled him in her arms rocking back and forth. "I love you," she said, kissing his head, caressing his face.

"Tell me... you love me... again," Jeremy said, squirming to breathe, to speak.

Natalie kissed Jeremy's lips, his cheek. She held his hand to her face. "Oh, God. Don't leave me. I love you," she said again.

"My beautiful Princess," he said, reaching up stroking her face. His arm dropped. He held his hand to her stomach. He struggled to breathe. "Promise... you'll name... our child... after me. It couldn't have all... been for nothing. I love you, Angel..."

Natalie draped herself over Jeremy as life dripped, poured out of him. Soaked with his blood, she cried from a pain so deep there would be nothing that would ever help her to heal. She had loved and lost so much, and there was still so much she wanted, needed to say to Jeremy, things she wanted to know. The few words they could share in these moments would never be enough to express how she felt, what she thought. To endure life without Jeremy was a sentence Natalie didn't want to face. "I love you," she said one final time. Tears cascaded down her cheeks. The spirit of the little girl that dwelled within her was severed. Her flame extinguished. She was alone. Her heart shattered. Just as the pure innocence of her youth had been taken. To live the rest of her life without the only man that made her feel loved, desired, worthy, whole—nothing could ever be the same.

Jeremy's body lay limp in her arms.

Natalie wished she were dead.

"He's down. We need medics. Have a gunshot wound," Detective Johnson said as her radio clicked with static.

"Read and copy. A unit's on its way," the voice on the other end replied.

BOOK II

THE RESURRECTION

Chapter Fifteen

Natalie clasped Jeremy's hand, as he lay motionless at Bellehaven Hospital. Her head on his lap. Bandages wrapped around his chest and back. The sun peeked in through the blinds of his room. An armed guard stood outside the door.

A plump nurse came in to adjust Jeremy's IV. "I'm sorry. You're going to have to leave," she said in a low voice. "We're not supposed to allow visitors for patients in police custody."

"I know," Natalie said somberly. "The guard was nice enough to let me have a few minutes with him. I'll go…" She held Jeremy's hand to her cheek then placed it by his side and left him. Natalie felt hollow inside, sad that she was alone, again, without Jeremy. She felt torn, not wanting to leave him abandoned, isolated. Natalie could not deny to herself in her private thoughts that she loved Jeremy, though a victim of his cruelty. She would rather have him hurt her than for him to not be in her life at all. His erratic behavior made her feel alive at her core.

Natalie was well acquainted with what it felt like to be a victim. Her father's icy temperament and brutal affronts had left her without an emotional imprint of how nurturing love from a man was supposed to feel. Her attempts to seek his approval and love had been met with verbal blows that destroyed her innate sense of goodness, intelligence, and beauty.

After two weeks in intensive care at Bellehaven, Jeremy was sent to Riker's Island. He had been charged with David's murder.

Sitting down slowly on the cold metal chair, Natalie pressed her right hand against the glass divider of the prisoner's visiting room. With her left hand, she lifted the phone receiver on the partition next to her.

Jeremy mirrored Natalie's hand, gingerly touching the glass that separated them. He grimaced in pain as he lifted his arm. He was still healing from the gunshot wound he had received.

They stared into each other's eyes in silence.

Natalie ached to be held by him, to turn back time, to make the pain she felt go away. She was tired, unable to sleep since Jeremy had been taken from her arms by the police into an ambulance.

"Thank you for coming," he said into the receiver, raising his voice to be heard over the din and chatter of the other inmates and their visitors.

"I spoke with my accountant and broker. We've arranged for you to have power of attorney. They're gonna get in contact with you to sign some papers. I need you to post my bail out of the money in the cash account…"

"…How did things get so messed up?" she asked.

"I don't know the answer to that. The only thing I know is that I never loved anyone the way I love you. I just want you all to myself, for us to live away from civilization in paradise forever and never look back. To kiss you…, to touch you…, to hold you…, to be in…" He looked to his left and right. "… just like we were in Cannes. That's all I ever wanted."

A tear rolled down Natalie's cheek. She dropped her head, unable to look into his eyes. It hurt too much.

"You are the most beautiful thing I have ever laid eyes on—a work of art… and you know, I'm a collector."

They both smiled a little.

"You have to help me get out of here. I want us to be together. The only thing that's important is that we love one another. I've never stopped loving you, wanting you, craving you… I need you, Natalie… I think about you day and night… I'm so sorry for everything that's happened."

She yearned to be close to him.

"…How are you feeling?" Jeremy asked.

"I have a little morning sickness but I'm okay the rest of the day." Natalie hung her head and then looked at Jeremy again. "I don't want to raise this baby without you."

"I don't want that either."

Natalie placed her forehead on the glass between them and closed her eyes. She loved Jeremy and nothing else mattered.

A loud bell sounded.

Natalie was startled.

"You're gonna have to leave," Jeremy said.

She felt helpless, that there wasn't anything in her control. Her world was moving in ways she didn't understand. It was like being fifteen again, where only the adults around her were in command and empowered to make the decisions. Natalie wanted to be with Jeremy, to feel safe in his arms, protected, to leave her complicated life behind.

"They have no real evidence against me," Jeremy said. "Only the circumstantial facts that I love you and was upset about your marriage."

"I know," Natalie said, getting up from the chair.

"A good attorney can tear their case apart... When will I see you again?" he asked.

"When I have one." While looking over her shoulder, her eyes fixed on Jeremy, a guard escorted her out.

In his baggy prison garb, Jeremy stood watching her leave him.

Natalie got in her car and drove to her parents in Westchester. When she pulled into the driveway, her mother poked her head through the lace dining room curtains and waved to her daughter. She was waiting by the door when Natalie walked in. They embraced. At that moment, they both needed reassurance and comforting.

"Daddy home?"

"He's in the study," her mother said, reluctantly. "I know why you're here. Natalie, don't do this."

"Mother, I have to. It's the only way Jeremy and I can be together."

"You're a beautiful girl. There are lots of other men out there."

"Not for me. There never was. This is who destiny chose for me to be with in this lifetime."

"You love him after everything, after all that he's put you through?" Betsy asked.

"Yes, I do. Please accept and support my decision, Mother. Please."

Betsy looked at her daughter with tears welling.

Natalie walked steadfastly down the long carpeted hallway she used to skip in. Her father was sitting at his majestic Louis XIV desk in a high back leather chair. She entered the study, shutting the double doors behind her. He removed his bifocals.

"Daddy, you have to represent him," Natalie said demurely.

"What?" Harv asked in astonishment.

"I need you to do this for me, Daddy," she insisted.

"Let me see if I have this right... This psycho rapes my daughter and then kills her husband and I should get him off? I always knew you were stupid, like your mother, but this really... Natalie, don't do this. He's no good... If you hadn't been such a whore, David would still be alive."

Natalie grimaced. "I'm sorry for what happened to David, but even if he were still alive, it wouldn't change the fact he was not right for me and that I didn't love him. I'm in this situation because of you, Daddy. If you hadn't been so God damned selfish thinking about the firm and not your flesh and blood, Jeremy never would have been able to..."

"So everything that's gone wrong in your life is my fault..."

"I've done everything you've asked me to my whole life, without question, even when I knew it was wrong for me. I went to that prep school because that's where your partner's kids went. I graduated from your damn alma mater because you wanted me to hang out with all the rich kids I couldn't stand for four years. I even married a total fucking asshole because it would be good for your practice. I'm asking you to do this one last thing. And I can promise you, I won't be around to ask you for anything else," she said, with a venomous hatred, teeth clenched.

Harv stood up and walked toward Natalie. "'Ms. Magna Cum Laude' should know it's a conflict of interest for me to..."

"Then get one of your 'friends' to do it."

"Again, with the friends. Forget it."

Natalie's mother hovered, listening to them argue through the closed doors. She burst in the room. "You do this for her, Harv," she shouted. "You owe her that much."

"Get the fuck outta here," he said, abusively shoving his wife.

"I'm walking right out that door—with Natalie—if you don't and I mean it," she said, recovering her balance.

Harv didn't say a word.

"C'mon," her mother said. "Let's go. You're wasting your time here, Natalie." They turned to walk out of the room.

"...Jesus fucking Christ... I'll give... Carl Jackman a call," Harv said reluctantly.

Natalie picked Jeremy up when he was released on bail. They drove in total silence for the hour car ride to the city. She brought Jeremy home to her apartment. When they arrived, John, the doorman, backed away as they walked into the lobby. He recognized Jeremy from the news and was shocked to see Natalie with him. A newspaper was sitting on the raised desk by the intercom. Natalie and Jeremy stared uncomfortably at the headline as they passed—'Park Grande Groom Murderer Released On Bail To Bride.'

"I guess you don't need a tour since you've been here before... just not with me," Natalie said entering the apartment.

"I've always been with you, baby. I think you know that now," he said, caressing her hair. "It's been a long ride. Can I use the bathroom?"

Natalie walked into the vanity area ahead of him. She had left in a hurry that morning and wanted to ensure it was in order.

Jeremy saw the mirror he had broken. "I'm sorry," he said. As he stood in back of her, they looked at their own cracked reflections. He began to kiss her neck. They started to make love on the vanity watching themselves in the distorted images of the broken mirror. He felt different to her. His touch—more sensitive. The way his body moved—more tender.

"You're making love to me, for the first time," she said. "This isn't sex anymore. Is it?"

"So perceptive. So in-tune... I can only act the way I feel... and I feel love."

Natalie drew Jeremy into her.

He consumed her.

They enveloped one another—each devouring every morsel of the other.

Natalie wanted to freeze time, to stay in this moment, suspended for eternity.

That evening, Natalie was preparing dinner while Jeremy showered. The phone rang.

"Did you see the paper today, Nat?" her father asked accusingly.

Being with him is bad for both of you—your reputation, your career," her father warned.

"I don't care about my reputation," she said defiantly.

"You're making things that much more difficult for his case, especially if it goes to trial," he hollered at Natalie. "She doesn't listen," Harv said to her mother, past the receiver.

"Something you have in common. How nice," Betsy muttered under her breath.

"How did you raise such a spoiled little girl?" he screamed.

"How did I marry such an ass, is more the question."

"Are you still there, Daddy?"

"Yeah. Your mother was being a bitch. What else is new?"

"Listen to me. We want to be together. This may be all the time we have and we're not gonna lose it. You can start by trying to get the charges dismissed. Find some technicality." She slammed the phone down hanging up on her father.

"I should probably go to work tomorrow," Natalie said, during their candle lit dinner.

Jeremy fidgeted with his fork and food. "I'll miss you…"

"…Maybe we can meet for lunch…" she suggested, breaking the awkward silence.

"Maybe you can be lunch," he said.

"I like the sound of that."

At work again the next day, Natalie felt isolated, ostracized by her colleagues. They glared at her as she moved through her day. Not a word was exchanged.

At noon Jeremy met Natalie in the lobby of her building. "I don't know if we're gonna be able to do this. They followed me all the way here," he said, motioning to the crowd outside the building.

They were mobbed by the press when they stepped outside—cameras flashing.

"Murderers," they heard someone scream.

They ducked back into the building quickly and ran into the stairwell, breathless. Jeremy abruptly pushed Natalie up against the wall, pinning her hands above her head. They kissed with a ravenous passion. She locked her legs around him. Then Natalie got down on her knees and unzipped Jeremy's trousers. She pleasured him orally, the sounds of chaos echoed from the other side of the steel door. Suddenly, they heard footsteps from above. Jeremy quickly put himself back into his pants. They heard a door squeak open overhead. The footsteps vanished. Their hearts were beating like teenagers making out on a couch hearing a parent's key in the door.

"You are amazing," Jeremy said, grinning. He loved how she always responded to his impassioned advances. Jeremy kissed her. "I don't want you to have to deal with what's going on out there. We'll have to finish this later..." He left to fight the mob scene alone.

Natalie walked up one flight to get the elevator back to her office avoiding another dose of the commotion.

"Nat, the guys in the penthouse are concerned about all the bad press you're bringing to SWA," Peter said, when she returned walking through the glass doors.

"Fine. Then I don't have to be here."

"Hold on there. No need to jump to conclusions, sweet cheeks. The first half of this year you pulled in more revenue than any of your comrades. All your clients are overseas and have no idea what's going on over here... Your buddy, Gunta, brought in seven figures alone... No, no, no..." he said, with a cajoling tone. "The 'big kahunas' are just looking for you to keep your scrumptious behind away from the paparazzi. Can you do that for Uncle Pete?"

"There's nothing I can do about it. This is what's going on in my life right now. And if it weren't for you being so fucking lazy and having me nurse your clients for you because your wife owns your balls, we all wouldn't be in this situation. Shall I tell that to the boys in the penthouse?"

"I don't think that'll be necessary. Glad to have you back. Keep up the good work. Nose to the grindstone whatnot and all that crap."

Late that afternoon, when Natalie went to the ladies room just before leaving her office, she received a phone message from Santiago. "Natalie, when you have some free time at home, call me on my private line. There are a few things I would like to discuss with you."

When Natalie returned home, Jeremy was only wearing a pair of faded Levi's. No shirt or shoes.

"Now where did we leave off earlier today?" she asked, tossing her bag down.

"Do me, baby."

Natalie whisked off her dress throwing it onto the floor. She stood there in a thong, push up bra, and four-inch heels.

Her cell phone rang.

"I better get it," she said, rummaging through her purse.

"Natalie. Did you get my message earlier?"

"I did but I was planning on calling you in the morning during your business day instead of your night. What's up, Enrique?"

Jeremy started to nibble on her neck and ear.

"We're interested in resurrecting the deal with JRMD but I want you to take the lead, Natalie. I don't want to deal with your boss. He's an idiot. And one other thing, I want you to come work for me afterwards and manage the transition. I'm prepared to offer you twice whatever you're making right now."

"But I thought…" she said, looking at Jeremy. "I'm very flattered. I guess I'll have to think about it. There's a lot going on right now."

"That's fine. Let me know when you've had an opportunity to meditate on it."

Natalie hung up, puzzled.

"So are you gonna take it?" Jeremy asked.

"You already knew about this?"

"Well, I didn't have a whole hell of a lot to do after I left you and dodged all those goons, so I called him up and told him I was still interested in buying up his electronics division. He's afraid I'm going to put his son out of business so I told him to hire you to keep me in line."

"But what if you…"

Jeremy touched her lips with his index finger softly to stop her from uttering another word. "Trust me. Your father is going to make this all go away, Princess."

"How can you be so sure?" Natalie asked.

"He knows we would torment him by disappearing… without a trace… otherwise. And you know how good I am at managing that. 'Daddy Dearest' doesn't want to lose his baby girl."

Natalie sat ruminating for a moment. "Holy shit. I could make a killing for SWA. How deliciously mischievous you've been today." She showered Jeremy with kisses on both his cheeks. Then stopped. A thought sprung from her memory. "Why did Enrique tell Pete I need to be careful of you?"

"Because I wanted to cut your boss out of the deal. He was concerned about the consequences career-wise for you. He's Pete's client. You come into the picture. Deal's off with him and on with you. He didn't want you to look bad just 'cause I'm greedy. That's all."

Natalie unzipped his pants and continued where they had left off earlier.

That night, while Natalie and Jeremy were lying in bed watching television, Adrian called. "What the fucking hell are you doing with your life?" she asked with an ice-cold air. "I turn on the news and see your face with that…"

"You and Daddy are always so supportive," Natalie replied in a monotone.

"Why can't you be normal for once?"

"Why can't you stop being jealous for once?"

"Oh yeah, I'm jealous of my sister who has a murdering rapist for a boyfriend… something to aspire to…"

Natalie sat up. "You have so much anger at yourself for making bad choices, you can't help taking it out on everyone around you. You were always mad that I chose to stay in shape and take care of myself. That I chose not to be financially dependent on Daddy or any other man. Just stop, A. You alienate everyone around you. Have you counted your friends lately?"

"And your choices are so much better?"

"The decisions I made for myself were the right ones—to go to grad school, to stay active physically—not eating my way to despair, to have a career and a commitment to be good at what I do. When I relied on those around me to make decisions for me, they weren't thinking about me. I'm only telling you this so we can both be happier in our own lives. If you want to continue to be angry at the world, I suppose that's a choice. Not a good one... I don't want to be angry. I don't want to be the victim any-more. I want to live a life I've chosen. Not one that someone else did... You make it so hard to love you, A... Are you hearing this at all?" By the time Natalie finished speaking, she heard only the buzz of the dial tone.

"Am I your choice?" Jeremy asked a while later as they lay in bed in the dark with only the glow of the streetlights below illuminating the room.

"Yes. In some way you always have been. I just didn't know it."

"And now...?"

Natalie turned to face him. "...I know it." She nestled her head into Jeremy's chest.

He held her tightly until they drifted off peacefully, comforted that the other was near. Natalie and Jeremy slept cuddling together.

Chuckles looked on contentedly, sitting propped up in the miniature rocking chair in the corner of the bedroom. He, too, was at peace, resting alone, not needed. How much burden could one bear take over a lifetime?

Chapter Sixteen

It was a crisp autumn morning. The leaves on the trees in Central Park were amber. Natalie stood staring out the window as daylight approached while Jeremy lay sleeping. At 6 AM the radio alarm went off.

"Top of the news this Monday morning, jurors will be selected in the Park Grande Hotel groom murder trial today."

With his eyes shut, Jeremy turned over and hit the off button on the clock radio. He reached out for Natalie but felt she was not by his side. Opening his eyes, he saw her at the window, arms folded, in a trance.

"Are you okay?" he asked.

Natalie looked back at him over her shoulder. "...Are you?" she asked, after a long pause.

Jeremy held his hand out, reaching for her to come to him.

Natalie sat on the edge of the bed—her head slung low.

He pushed her hair back out of her eyes and stroked her face.

She leaned down resting her head on his chest, listening to his heartbeat as he caressed her back.

"I need you to be there today for me, for us. There may be times when we can't tell the whole truth. It's the only way we'll be able to be together, as a family—you, me and our beautiful baby."

"I'm gonna go for a short run," Natalie said, feeling uneasy. "A couple of times around the reservoir, just to clear my head." She was anxious about the possibility of having to lie in order to be with Jeremy. But Natalie knew she did not want to live without him, to raise their child alone. She knew she had to do whatever it took to ensure their future together.

Jeremy watched her pull on a royal blue spandex unitard. With a contented gleam, he stared at her developing tummy.

Natalie kissed the top of his head and was off for her jog. When she got downstairs and tried to exit the building, she was bombarded by reporters and photographers snapping and clicking their cameras, barraging her with questions. She covered her eyes, unable to focus.

"Ms. Baylor, today's probably not a good day for a jog," Felix, the morning doorman, said trying to console her.

Natalie returned to her apartment, shaken.

"Is that you, baby?" Jeremy called to her.

She walked into the bedroom and opened the window. "Look

outside."

Jeremy peered out. "I'm sorry you had to deal with that," he said, hugging her.

They showered and dressed in silence.

A few minutes before seven, Natalie had her usual bout of morning nausea and vomiting. The ringing of the telephone startled her. She wiped and rinsed her mouth with cool tap water to answer the phone.

"We're downstairs," her mother said, calling on her cell phone from the car. "There are tons of reporters swarming around."

Natalie cleared her throat. "I know. You need to have Daddy go around the block and pick us up at the service entrance in back. There's no other way to do this without being bombarded. We'll be right down." She grabbed a package of crackers from the kitchen cupboard to calm her stomach and tossed them in her purse.

Her father drove the four of them to the courthouse downtown in his olive Benz. Jeremy held Natalie's hand. Harv focused intently on navigating through the rush hour traffic, not wanting to be late. Betsy reached for the radio dial to turn on the news. Harv motioned to her not to. No one spoke. They parked in the lot adjacent to the courthouse. Reporters mobbed them as they made their way up the stairs. Jeremy had his arm around Natalie. Her parents walked close behind.

"Natalie, did you have Jeremy kill your husband so you could be together?" one bold reporter shouted over the noise of the crowd.

Harv grabbed the reporter's press badge, reading his name. "Shut the fuck up, Jim Haynes from WHQV, or I'll see that your fat ass is unemployed."

They went through the revolving doors, the metal detector, and security check. Adrian was waiting for them when they entered the lobby. They proceeded to the elevators to meet with Carl Jackman in a small room on the third floor next to the courtroom.

"Baby, before we head on in, I just want to have a word with your dad, to thank him for... well, you go on in," Jeremy said to Natalie.

"Harv, can we talk for a minute..." Jeremy put his hand on his shoulder. "I can call you Harv," he suggested with a snide tone. "We're practically family. I just want to be clear from the outset where we stand with one another, Harv. Communication in a relationship is so important, you know."

"What is it, you pompous prick?"

"Here's the deal," Jeremy said, in a hushed voice. "If you don't get your 'boys' to do this job right, I'll get one of mine to kill Natalie. You already tried to take her away from me once and I'll be God damned if I'm gonna rot away in 'the Pen' while she's on the outside fucking some other guy. Man to man, I'm sure you can understand that. Can't you, Harv? ...And let me tell you, she can give one hell of a ride. So, your buddy, Carl,

better pull a win out of his ass. I hope I'm making myself perfectly clear."
Jeremy walked away.

Harv was left unable to utter a word or throw back one of his can-tankerous, degrading insults though his blood boiled from anger. For the first time, concern for his daughter was at the forefront of his thoughts.

Jeremy sat at the defense table conferring with Carl and his three co-counsel. Natalie, Adrian, and their parents sat in the last row of the gallery behind Jeremy. The District Attorney, Ned Billings, a pasty-faced young man wearing glasses from the seventies and a cheap beige suit, filed in with an expandable leather briefcase in each hand. They were over-stuffed, bulging. An anorexic-looking female assistant carried an over-flowing armful of papers. The stenographer set up her machine in front of the judge's bench.

"All rise for the Honorable Justice George T. Maxwell," a court officer announced. "Superior Court of the State of New York is now in session."

Standing up, Jeremy turned to look back at Natalie. Her stomach was churning. Another wave of nausea swept over her. She started to sweat, her face ashen. Natalie's mother and sister each took one of her hands to comfort her.

"Is the State ready to proceed?" the judge asked.

"Yes, Your Honor," the D.A. replied.

Judge Maxwell peered over his bifocals. "And the defense, Mr. Jackman?"

"We are, Your Honor."

"Then let's get started. Bring in the first pool of jurors, please," the judge said, motioning to the court officer.

After three days of voir dire, the jury was finally assembled. The Thursday morning that the trial was to begin, Natalie and Jeremy met with Carl at the courthouse at 8 AM to prepare Natalie to testify.

"I shouldn't be talking to you about your testimony, Natalie," Carl said. "But I know I can trust you. Jeremy does. Both sides are going to present their opening remarks, what we each set out to prove or disprove. Natalie, you're the prosecution's star witness. Without your testimony, the entire case is based on circumstantial evidence and there's not enough here to convict Jeremy of murder. He can't be placed at the scene of the crime unless you tell them with certainty that he confessed to you he killed David, how your necklace got in David's hand when you found him dead, that you had given it to Jeremy, or anything else incriminating that would implicate him. Without a rape kit, they're not going to be allowed to bring in anything concrete against Jeremy for your rape without your positive identification of him. The prosecution can't make the correlation that the murder weapon and the knife used during the rape were the same without you. Jeremy's fingerprints were not found on it or at the scene where David was killed. It's all up to you, Natalie. The D.A.'s case hinges on your testimony. Their strategy will be to put those individuals up on the stand that will corroborate what you say to implicate him. Stay calm. Give me time to object if I think it's warranted. Don't answer more than what you've been asked. Try to use 'yes' or 'no' responses as much as possible. The more you give them, the more they'll dig and we don't want that. Any questions?"

"Will he be taking the stand?" Natalie asked, looking at Jeremy.

"Not if we can help it," Jackman said. "Even though you're a witness for the prosecution, I think you're gonna do a great job for us and we won't need Jeremy's testimony."

When they walked out of their private conference, Natalie's parents were waiting outside the room.

Harv pulled Carl aside. "You need to do whatever it takes to win this one, Carl. I'm serious."

"You know we'll do our best."

"No, you need to get this guy off no matter what. He has to walk out of here a free man. There is no other option. Do you understand me?"

"Harv, you seem a little off kilter. It's gonna be okay. The State's case is all circumstantial. You know how weak that is. And the jury'll find

Natalie credible."

"That gnat of a D.A. is going to tear her to shreds."

"Yeah, he probably will, but she's a strong young lady. She's your daughter right? And besides, if she wants to be with this guy, she'll... We've prepped her. That's all I can say."

Natalie sat very still in the back of the courtroom during the opening remarks. Her stomach quivered when the D.A. called Detective Johnson.

"Please state your full name and affiliation for the record," the court clerk said.

"Detective Renee Sisley Johnson of the fourteenth precinct, New York City Police Department."

She was sworn in.

"How did you come to know the defendant?" the D.A. asked.

"I was one of the officers called to the scene at the Park Grande Hotel where a Mr. David Hughes was mortally wounded and then led the subsequent murder investigation involving the defendant."

"And Ms. Baylor?"

"She was at the scene when I arrived."

"How did you identify Jeremy Dalton as the individual that killed David Hughes?"

"I over heard Ms. Baylor tell my C.O…"

"C.O.?"

"I'm sorry… my Commanding Officer, Lieutenant Grealy, that she knew who had killed her husband and that it was Mr. Dalton."

"Were there any circumstances leading up to her telling your 'C.O.' this?"

"She believed that Mr. Dalton had just attempted to kill her mother and Ms. Baylor was in fear for her own safety…"

"What did you do when you overheard Ms. Baylor tell your 'C.O.' that she thought Jeremy killed her husband?"

"I attempted to get her to tell me why she thought that."

"Objection. This is all hearsay, Your Honor," Jackman said.

"Overruled."

"Judge…"

"Approach."

"It's Ms. Baylor's admissions to police that directed the investigation to Mr. Dalton," the D.A. said quietly.

"Understood, but the State does need to bring that out through additional means other than just what Ms. Baylor has said," the judge replied. "Will the prosecution be doing that any time soon?"

"Yes, Your Honor."

"Proceed."

"Did Ms. Baylor share any additional information with you direct-ly to support her statement?"

"She talked about a necklace of hers that Jeremy had—the one that David was holding when he was murdered."

The D.A. handed the officer a small plastic bag that contained a gold chain with a small cross hanging from it. "Is this the necklace, Detective?"

Jeremy was stoic. Motionless.

"Yes it is."

Harv, sitting in the back, looked down. His chest tight. He, too, was familiar with the necklace.

"I'd like the necklace marked into evidence as 'people's exhibit one.' Did Ms. Baylor state how Mr. Dalton had come into possession of the necklace and later Mr. Hughes?"

"Ms. Baylor stated she had given the necklace to Mr. Dalton."

The blood vessels in Harv's head felt like they were going to explode any moment.

Carl conferred with his co-counsel. "Objection. Can this witness provide any direct evidence relevant to this case? The detective's only tes-timony has been what Ms. Baylor may have stated. I move to strike this witness's testimony."

"Your objection is overruled, counselor. But Mr. Billings, let's move on or I will instruct the jury to disregard anything further."

The D.A. was looking down at some papers on his desk.

"Did the police take any further action to obtain additional information?"

"Yes. We put a tap on her phone to pick up any contact between Ms. Baylor and Mr. Dalton."

"And what did you find?"

"We did not detect any direct communication, but again Ms. Baylor stated that the defendant had contacted her..."

"Your Honor," Jackman interrupted.

"I'm done with this witness at this time," the D.A. said sheepishly.

"Your witness, Mr. Jackman," the judge said.

"Thank you, Your Honor. Good morning, Detective Johnson... Did you find Mr. Dalton's fingerprints on the murder weapon?"

"No."

"Did you find Mr. Dalton's fingerprints, DNA, or any other forensic evidence at the murder scene, in the Park Grande Hotel suite where Mr. Hughes and Ms. Baylor had been staying?"

"No, I did not."

"Was Mr. Dalton on any of the hotel lobby surveillance video tapes the police viewed in connection with this investigation showing the defendant entering or exiting the hotel the morning Mr. Hughes was murdered? Does the police have any direct evidence whatsoever that my client was at the Park Grande Hotel the day of the murder?"

"No," the detective said hesitantly.

"I have nothing further for this witness," Jackman said.

"The witness may step down," the judge said. "The State will call its next witness."

Natalie walked to the witness stand trying to remain composed though her stomach was churning.

"State your full name for the record," the court clerk said.

"Natalie Anne Baylor," she said timidly.

She was sworn in.

"You're going to have to speak up so the jury can hear you," the judge said.

Natalie nodded.

"Ms. Baylor, can you tell us, in your own words, what transpired the morning you found your husband murdered?" the D.A. asked.

Jeremy watched Natalie intently.

"I woke up around eight, showered and packed for my honeymoon."

"Where was your husband?"

"He was still in bed."

"How would you describe his appearance at that time?"

"He was groggy. Maybe a little hung over from the wedding festivities."

"After you packed, then what did you do?"

"I realized I didn't have my purse from the night before. I called Inn on the Park, where we had the reception, and the manager said that it had been given to my mother. She was staying just a few blocks from the Park Grande Hotel, where David and I were, so I told him I was going to go pick up my bag from her."

"How long were you gone?"

"About an hour. My mother and I had a little breakfast and I left in a hurry to get back to the hotel. I didn't want us to miss our flight."

"And when you returned to the hotel, can you tell us what happened?"

"I opened the door to our room and..." Natalie looked down and took a deep breath. "...and I saw David... hanging from the chandelier, naked, blood dripping down his legs. He had a switchblade in his chest. He'd been stabbed." The memory of David's body shook her.

"At this time, Your Honor, I would like to enter the knife found in the victim as 'people's exhibit two,'" the D.A. requested.

"So noted," the judge replied.

"Did you recognize the knife that was used to kill your husband?" he asked, holding up a zip lock sandwich bag with a red-handled switchblade in it.

"No," Natalie said. Looking into Jeremy's eyes, she remembered her rape and the first time she saw the knife.

"Had you seen this knife before the day your husband was stabbed?"

"Objection! The witness has answered the question," Jackman said.

"Sustained," the judge said.

"Request sidebar, Your Honor," the D.A. said.

The judge motioned for counsel to approach. He covered his microphone so the jury wouldn't hear their private discussion.

"Your Honor, the defendant used the knife during the rape of the witness," the D.A. said in a hushed voice. "She has seen it before."

"And under cross, the witness will be providing testimony regarding the loss of her memory due to injuries sustained to her head when she was raped as a teenager," Jackman whispered.

The judge uncovered his microphone. "Move on, counsel," he said to the District Attorney.

The D.A. appeared flustered, uncertain. He returned to the prosecutor's table and shuffled some papers for a moment before continuing to confront Natalie. "Ms. Baylor, the investigating officer has already testified that your husband was holding a necklace in his hand. Did you recognize it?"

"Yes. It was mine."

How did it end up in his hand at the time you found him dead?"

"I don't know," Natalie said, glancing at Jeremy and Jackman as they leaned forward to hear her.

"Where had you seen it last?"

"I don't remember."

The D.A. paused to look down at his notes. He appeared uncertain. "Did you know the defendant at the time your husband was killed?"

"Yes. We were business associates."

"Were you anything else?"

"Objection," Jackman said. "Irrelevant."

"Overruled. The witness will answer."

"Were you and the defendant something other than just business associates?"

"Yes."

"Were you lovers?"

"Yes."

"You had been having an affair for how long before your husband was murdered?"

Natalie looked away, hesitant to answer. "It was on a business trip. It lasted only a few days."

Betsy turned away. She couldn't bear listening to her daughter reveal something so personal in such a public forum.

"Did your feelings for the defendant last for only a few days?"

Natalie was hesitant to answer watching her mother squirm. "...No."

"Did you tell David, your fiancé at the time, of your feelings for another man?"

Natalie was getting upset, angry. "No."

Harv wiped the sweat on his forehead.

"You stated that your affair with the defendant lasted only a few days. Weeks later you were seen on lobby surveillance cameras at the Hotel Royale and then taking the elevator to a floor that had only a private suite in which the defendant was staying."

Natalie saw her father in the back of the courtroom writhing with disgust.

"I didn't know I was to meet him that day at the hotel. My boss referred to him as JR. At that time, I didn't know the defendant by any name other than Jeremy Dalton."

"But you went up to his room nonetheless?"

"Yes, to discuss a business matter."

"According to hotel surveillance tapes, you left the next morning. You were there simply to discuss a business matter?" the D.A. asked with an accusatory tone.

"Objection," Jackman said, bolting out of his chair.

"Withdrawn... Did you come to know him by any other names at any point later on?"

Jeremy and Jackman were whispering to each other.

Natalie was becoming visibly uncomfortable. "Yes. I later found out his full name."

"Ms. Baylor, the defendant's legal name is Jeremy Robert McDonough Dalton. Did you ever know a Robert McDonough?"

"Yes."

"And who was he?"

She fidgeted in her chair. "He worked in an ice cream parlor I had gone to after school as a child." Natalie's head throbbed. She pictured Jeremy behind the counter serving her and Megan. She felt her heart race. In her mind, she was running through the woods. She looked at Jeremy sitting across from her, then saw visions of him looming over her, hurting her, thrusting himself into her again and again.

"So you knew the defendant before. Ms. Baylor, do you recognize the defendant from anywhere else?" the prosecutor asked insistently, almost shouting.

Natalie couldn't answer. She had shooting pains in her stomach, a look of panic on her face. Her eyes, haunted with agony, met her mother's. She clutched at her mid-section.

"Oh, God. Something's wrong with the baby," Betsy said to Adrian.

"Your Honor, please instruct the witness to answer the question." the D.A. demanded, ignoring Natalie's distracted, disturbing demeanor.

"The witness will answer the question," the judge insisted.

"I repeat, do you recognize the defendant from anywhere else, Ms. Baylor," the D.A. demanded.

"No!" Natalie shouted, almost doubled over from pain.

Jackman bolted up from his chair. "I request a ten minute recess, Your Honor. The witness is obviously in some sort of physical distress."

"So granted."

The jury was escorted out. Jeremy and Carl helped Natalie down from the stand. Her mother rushed to her side.

"Mother, something's wrong," Natalie said with tears welling in her eyes. "I don't want to lose this baby."

"Christ almighty," Jeremy exclaimed. "She's bleeding." The back of her skirt was soaked with blood.

"Jesus. We have to get her to a hospital," Carl said.

"I want to go with her," Jeremy said.

"There's no way. You're on trial here. The show must go on, I'm afraid. Maybe we can get the judge to order the prosecution to call their next witness. I can cross-examine her later."

"Carl, you better figure something out here," Harv said.

Natalie winced in pain.

"Adrian, call 911 on your cell phone," Betsy insisted.

It only took a few minutes for the paramedics to arrive. Natalie was taken to the emergency room at Manhattan Methodist Downtown. Her mother went with her in the ambulance. When they got to the hospital, after a long wait for the triage nurse to get to her, Natalie was bombarded with a long series of questions about her pain while her pulse, temperature, and blood pressure were taken. Moments later, a female technician with a Jamaican accent, wheeled her to radiology where she was prepped for a vaginal and external sonogram. A cold wand covered with gel was inserted into Natalie and the technician moved it around exploring inside her for several uncomfortable minutes. Natalie's mother patted her head. The wand was removed. Gel was squeezed onto her slightly rounded stomach. The technician made circular motions with the scanning device over her abdomen.

"Oh, my God, Natalie. Look," her mother said.

The technician turned the screen so Natalie could see. "I think you're having a boy."

"Is he going to be okay?" Natalie asked with concern.

A man in a white coat came in the room at that moment. "I'm Dr. Samuels. Let me have a look here." He took the technician's seat and continued to move the wand over Natalie's stomach. "We're going to need to run a few more tests to see if he's okay... but it does look like it's a boy," the doctor said to Natalie. "Let's get an amnio going right away," he said to the technician.

"Please don't let me lose this baby," Natalie said, overwrought, distress clouding her eyes.

Chapter Seventeen

After the end of the first day of the trial, Harv drove Jeremy and Adrian to the hospital when court recessed. Jeremy rushed through the door of Natalie's room to be at her side.

Betsy stepped out to let them be alone.

"How are you?" Jeremy asked, patting her head.

"I'm okay...," Natalie said, despondently. "I'm sorry I let you down... When I was sitting there... I didn't want to lie but I knew if I didn't... I just don't know who you are sometimes. Are you Robert who hurt me very badly?... Or are you Jeremy who I love more than anything?"

Jeremy looked down and thought for a moment. "...I guess I'm both. I loved you so much. I thought you were so beautiful—like an angel. I was infuriated that you never noticed me because I wasn't someone... We know you never would have given me the time of day if I hadn't made something of myself. We've both hurt each other... You and I, we're not that different. We both crave love, passion, romance... That's why we feel the way we do about one another. That's why we have the incredible attraction and fire we have for each other. But we also know pain, self-hate, and anger—what it's like to have a selfish, egotistical father and a good-intentioned though spineless mother. We're kindred spirits, Angel. When you fall, I bleed. We are one... You could never let me down..." Jeremy held her. "How's... the baby?"

"Jeremy Junior is going to be fine," Natalie said.

With a look of relief, he pressed his forehead against Natalie's. "It's a boy," he said, with joy on his face.

Natalie caressed his hair, inhaling the scent of his cologne. She loved being loved by him.

Betsy and Harv were outside Natalie's room.

"Carl couldn't get the judge to agree to move forward without a cross-examination of Natalie," Harv said.

"We can't let her go through anymore of that," Betsy said. "The doctor told us she has to stay away from stress."

"Would you let me finish?" Harv snapped. "Carl said the D.A. agreed to consider their questioning of Natalie complete if Jeremy takes the stand for the defense and they can cross-examine him. She'll get up there.

The little weasel of a D.A. will say he has no additional questions for this witness. Then Carl'll ask her about her memory loss and then say he has nothing further for this witness but reserve the right to further question her later and she's done. He thought the jury might view anything that she may have already said as having little relevance as a result and would then ben-efit the defense. I don't know..." Beads of sweat were collecting on his brow. "It just makes things tougher when you have a completely guilty defendant take the stand."

"Harv, are you okay?" Betsy asked, with concern.

"No, I'm not okay," he said, slowly sitting down in a chair in the lounge. He rested his head in his hands and began to weep uncontrollably.

"I've never seen you like this before," she said.

Dr. Samuels walked toward them down the long, icy corridor.

Harv wiped his face.

"We're going to keep her overnight for observation. She should be able to go home tomorrow morning. But you need to help her stay away from anything that could upset her or we'll all be back here again and maybe not so lucky."

Two days later, Lieutenant Grealy testified that he could not remember the details of his conversation with Natalie the day she and her mother went to the police station together. The D.A. questioned the

223

coroner about David's death. He made it clear that David had died from strangulation when he was hanged from the chandelier and was stabbed shortly thereafter. Carl had no questions for either witness. The D.A. rested the State's case.

"We call Jeremy Dalton," Carl said.

Jeremy moved confidently across the courtroom to take his place in the witness chair.

"Please state your full name for the record," the court clerk said.

"Jeremy Robert McDonough Dalton."

He was sworn in.

Harv sat in the back of the gallery, his heart racing.

"Can you tell us where you were the morning David Hughes was murdered?" Jackman asked.

"I was staying at the Hotel Royale. I was in New York for a few days on business."

"Were you alone that morning?"

"Yes. I had breakfast in my room, read the paper, showered and then met a colleague, Cal Reynolds, for lunch." Jeremy had a smug look on his face.

"The hotel records stated you had breakfast brought to your room at 8 AM. What time did you meet your colleague for lunch?"

"Noon."

"At any time from eight o'clock to noon that day did you go to the Park Grande Hotel?"

"No," Jeremy answered emphatically, staring directly at the jury.

"I have no further questions for Mr. Dalton."

The D.A. stood up buttoning his jacket. "Are you in love with Natalie Baylor?"

"Yes."

"Were you in love with her the day David Hughes was brutally murdered?"

"Yes."

"Is this you, Mr. Dalton, standing in the picture—in the back of the garden of Inn on the Park at the wedding of David Hughes and Natalie Baylor—the day before Mr. Hughes' murder?"

"Objection," Jackman said. "Sidebar, Your Honor."

The judge motioned for the two attorneys to approach.

"The defense knows of no such photos," Carl said.

"How were these photos obtained?" the judge asked.

"The police subpoenaed the wedding photographer who furnished copies of the photos."

"The witness will answer," the judge said.

"Yes, it is."

Natalie's mother covered her mouth as she gasped.

"At this time I would like to enter this photo into evidence as 'people's exhibit three,' Your Honor." The D.A. handed the photo to the court clerk to be marked.

"Mr. Dalton, were you an invited guest to Ms. Baylor and Mr. Hughes' wedding?"

"No, I was not."

"Can you tell us why you were there?"

"It was just something I felt I needed to do."

"Were you upset or angry as you watched the woman you stated that you loved marry another man?"

"I was not happy about it."

"Did it make you jealous?"

"I wouldn't say jealous."

"What would you say?"

"That I was not happy about it."

The D.A. sat down at the prosecutor's table.

"Re-direct, Your Honor," Jackman said. "Because you were not 'happy' about your lover marrying another man, did you kill him? Did you murder David Hughes?"

"No, I did not," Jeremy said looking at the jury.

Carl questioned Cal Reynolds who confirmed Jeremy had lunch with him at noon the day David was killed. Cal stated Jeremy had no bruises, cuts, or scrapes at that time that he could see.

Carl made his closing statements. "You can't find my client guilty because the State has not met its burden of proof. It's just that simple. No physical evidence links Jeremy Dalton to the murder. He was not on any of the Park Grande Hotel's surveillance videotapes the morning of David's murder. As for the police's accusation that Ms. Baylor said Jeremy murdered her husband—one officer stated that Natalie said that and the other officer didn't know whether she did or not. The D.A. could not substantiate that accusation without leaving reasonable doubt that Ms. Baylor said that or not. The police did not consider any other suspects. David had ordered room service just before he was killed. A member of the hotel's staff was the last one to see Mr. Hughes alive. That's who should be on trial here today…" He took his seat next to Jeremy.

The D.A. approached the juror's box, resting his hands on the wooden ledge. "This trial has been a mockery, ladies and gentlemen. I know it and you know it. You heard the defendant lie to you. You heard his lover lie to you. Jeremy Dalton wanted David Hughes out of the way so that he and his lover, Natalie Baylor, could be together. He stated he was not 'happy' about his lover marrying another man to the point where he stalked Ms. Baylor and Mr. Hughes at their own wedding. His whereabouts are uncertain for nearly four hours the morning David Hughes was brutally murdered. No one else had the motive to kill David Hughes. You know that Jeremy Dalton is guilty..."

The jury was sequestered for forty-eight hours, returning each day to have testimony read and re-read to them as well as the definitions of murder in the first degree and reasonable doubt.

When Jackman received word that the jury had reached a verdict, he called Natalie at home where she was waiting nervously. "They're ready. Get in a cab right away. I'll hold them off as long as I can."

Natalie had not been back to the courthouse since she had completed her testimony the day after she was in the hospital. It would have been too much for her and Jeremy Junior. Natalie was able to get a taxi immediately. There were no members of the press outside her building. They were all congregating at the courthouse. The cab raced down the West Side Highway and got her to the courthouse in twenty worrisome minutes. Natalie arrived just as the jury was filtering into the courtroom. She snuck into the back row of the gallery to sit with her parents and sister. Natalie noticed Detective Johnson was seated on the opposite side of the room in the back row.

Their eyes met.

Natalie turned away.

"None of the jurors are looking at him, Jesus Christ," Harv said, in a hushed voice to Betsy.

Natalie's mother took her daughter's hand.

The court officer handed the judge a slip of paper.

"Madame Foreperson, have you reached a verdict?"

"Yes, Your Honor. We have."

"Will the defendant please rise," the judge said. "What say you in the matter of the people of the State of New York versus Jeremy Robert McDonough Dalton?"

Jeremy looked back and saw Natalie. "Love you," he mouthed to her.

She was holding her breath, her heart racing.

"We find the defendant..."

Natalie's mother was clasping her hand so tightly the tips of her fingers began to tingle.

"...not guilty."

"The defendant is free to go," the judge said, and smacked his gavel down.

Natalie exhaled.

Adrian hugged her sister, lingering for several moments. "Do what you need to do, Nat, if this is your choice. Just be happy. Please, please be careful."

Jeremy stood up and shook Carl's hand. "You did a great job. Thank you."

Harv patted the sweat on his forehead with a white handkerchief from the chest pocket of his suit, not certain if he did the right thing by helping his daughter's rapist remain free a second time.

Betsy was dumbstruck, emotionless—afraid of what would happen to her daughter now. She began to tremble, realizing Natalie was going to be with a sinister rapist capable of murdering in cold-blood and that she had helped make this happen. Natalie's mother never thought Jeremy would be found innocent. She just wanted to show support for her daughter in love, making her own decisions. Betsy felt as if she had again failed to protect her baby girl from harm. She had thrust her into the arms of the devil himself. Terror filled her eyes as she watched her daughters pulling back from their embrace.

Detective Johnson walked over to Natalie. "If this is what you want, Natalie, I wish you luck. But if this guy becomes a problem, you know where to find me."

Natalie didn't know whether to thank her for her offer or unleash her anger for shooting Jeremy and nearly taking him from her. So she said nothing—almost looking through the officer as if she wasn't there.

When Natalie and Jeremy were coming out of the courthouse with her parents, the press and public hounded them, barely letting them get one foot in front of the other to walk back to the garage. Reporters, angry at the verdict, were screaming insults at them.

When Harv turned onto Central Park West as he drove Natalie and Jeremy home, they could see a small crowd in front of her apartment building.

Natalie and Jeremy realized silently they wouldn't be able to establish a life and live quietly together in New York.

"Good-bye, Daddy," Natalie said, piercing the memory of his face in her mind as she and her mother got out of the car.

Jeremy extended his hand to Harv.

He did not reciprocate the gesture. "You so much as give her a paper cut, and I will kill you. Do we understand one another?"

Standing on the sidewalk, Natalie and her mother hugged each other. Tears ran down both their faces. Neither wanted to let the other go.

Betsy knew this would be the last time they would be together—a way only a mother could understand. "Honey, you know I'll support you whatever you feel you need to do..." her mother said, stroking Natalie's hair, weeping. "...But I'm afraid for you, Natalie... I love you... You'll always be my little girl... You can always come home..."

"I'm gonna be okay, Mother... For the first time, I think I'm gonna be okay."

The press swarmed around them with cameras and microphones. With the world watching, they said a secret good-bye.

When Natalie and Jeremy got upstairs, Natalie called Santiago. "I'll accept your offer on one condition," she said. "Do you have a good ob/gyn over there?"

"My son and daughter-in-law just had their second. I'm sure you'll be in good hands."

"I'll execute the contract for the sale and fax it over. It just needs your signature."

"Natalie, this thrills me. Welcome aboard."

When Natalie received the signed contract back from Santiago she dialed Peter and put him on the speaker phone so she could type on her laptop.

"Hey, Nat. I get a hard on just seeing your phone number pop up on my screen."

Jeremy scowled at Natalie.

She stayed focused, ignoring Peter's comment. "Enrique called me. He wants to go through with the sale to JRMD."

"Sweet. This is big bucks," Peter said.

"He wants me to lead the deal."

Pete was silent.

"I'll split the 'commish' with you fifty-fifty," she said.

"You did all the work for it—on your back... Well, what with the trial and all, I guess you deserve it."

Again, Jeremy had a look of disdain at Peter's sexually-charged remarks to Natalie.

"Enrique faxed me his signed copy of the contract. I'll shoot you a copy. We're done here." Natalie tapped a few keys on her computer. "Hey, Pete. Check your email."

"...You're fucking kidding me? God I'll miss that tight little ass of yours. Shit. This means I'll have to deal with Gunta."

"See you on the other side." Natalie had resigned.

As soon as Natalie had disconnected the call, Jeremy stood over her, drew his arm back, and slammed her face with his hand. "I don't ever want to hear another guy talk to you like that ever again. Do you understand me, Angel?"

Natalie clutched her face. Blood dripped from her bottom lip onto her fingers.

Jeremy grabbed her hand inserting her blood-soaked fingers, one-by-one, into his mouth sucking the crimson fluid away. He kissed Natalie's swollen lips.

She winced.

He kissed her neck, unbuttoning her blouse.

Natalie ran her fingers through his hair softly and then pulled at it hard yanking his head back.

"Bitch!" Jeremy yelled out and smacked Natalie again. He straddled her on the floor, pinning her hands above her head.

Natalie was afraid but her fear aroused her. She could feel Jeremy was hard pressing against her. "Fuck me, you bastard," she screamed.

And he did.

Natalie wailed in ecstasy to the rhythm of his pelvic gyrations. When Jeremy kissed the open gash on her lips, Natalie cringed. She could not distinguish pain from pleasure. Natalie craved every inch of his flesh. It would take a lifetime to satisfy her hunger for Jeremy, if ever. She thrived on the passion he felt for her. It fed her starving soul.

Jeremy made erotic love to Natalie until the sun's piercing light broke through darkness.

The next morning, Natalie and Jeremy packed what they could manage to fit into two small suitcases. Natalie wrapped a silk kerchief around her head and donned large-rimmed black sunglasses. Jeremy wore a wide-brimmed hat and over-sized sunglasses. They didn't want to be recognized. Just before they left the apartment, he reached for Natalie's hand.

"I don't think you'll be needing this any more," Jeremy said, sliding off her finger the engagement ring and wedding band David had given her. He placed them in her other palm. From his coat pocket he pulled out a small black velvet jewelry box with a three-carat diamond ring inside and put it on her ring finger.

Natalie opened her jewelry box and dropped David's rings in as the tiny chimes sounded. She did not wince at the tinkling. There were no horrific scenes spiraling through her head.

They embraced, kissing. Their mouths engulfed one another.

Nothing made Natalie happier than knowing she was loved by Jeremy. She reached into her carry-on bag sitting on the bed and pulled Chuckles out. She looked at him lovingly and delicately placed him back on the small rocking chair in the corner of her bedroom. Natalie was at peace for the first time since she and Megan had shared their cups of ice cream.

A limousine was waiting for them when they got downstairs. As they drove along the park, the city Natalie knew so well seemed unfamiliar to her. It no longer felt like her home.

When they arrived at JFK, the driver dropped them at different curbside entrances at the international terminal.

Natalie walked to the gate for their flight and got on line to check in.

Jeremy then appeared on line in back of her.

They did not acknowledge each other.

When she got to the counter, Natalie handed the ticket agent her passport.

After opening the passport and looking at the photo and name, the representative at the counter did a double take of her and then at Jeremy standing behind her.

"Is there any room in first class?" Natalie asked, sliding her sunglasses down the bridge of her nose.

The ticket agent was immobile for, what seemed to Natalie, an interminable minute.

"Would you and Mr. Dalton like to sit together?" she asked, with no emotion leaning in to Natalie.

Natalie slid her glasses back on. "Yes. We would. Thank you."

"I have you in 3A, Ms. Baylor."

Natalie left the counter to find a seat in the lounge.

Jeremy smiled at Natalie as she passed.

She returned the smile, walking past him.

His eyes drop to admire her gym-tightened glutes.

"I have you seated in first with Ms. Baylor," the ticket agent said.

"Great. Thanks." He took the seat next to Natalie in the waiting area. "So, how long are you going to be in Paris?" he asked playfully.

"Just for one night and then I fly to Nice, but I'll be staying in Cannes. And you?" she asked, with a smirk.

"I have some business to attend to in Paris but I have a small beach home in the south that I'm headed to."

"Oh, that sounds great."

"Come on along."

Natalie was silent though her interest was piqued.

Jeremy felt her hesitation and quickly changed the subject. "So what do you do when you're not in airports?"

"I was an investment banker on Wall Street."

"Beautiful *and* smart. And I would imagine very comfortable financially too. Not bad."

Natalie smiled. "And what do you do?"

"I'm an investor for the most part. I buy and sell real estate, art, business concerns. I like to acquire things. Whatever makes sense. Whatever interests me."

"Right now we would like to begin boarding Flight 1054 non-stop to Paris..." they heard over the loud speaker.

"Looks like they're boarding. Where are you sitting?"

"3A," Natalie said.

"You mean I have the honor of sitting next to you all the way to the 'City of Lights.' How did I get so lucky?" When they started walking toward the jet way, Jeremy put his arm around her back. He looked her up and down soaking in the view.

She caught him and laughed.

"Busted. Just admiring a beautiful work of art. It's what I do. And a work of art you are."

They walked through the ramp onto the plane and to their seats.

"Let me help you with that," Jeremy said, placing her bag in the overhead compartment. "Anything you need out of here?"

"No. I've got my book in my purse. Thanks."

They settled into their seats.

"So let me see what your reading."

She reached into her bag and handed him a paperback.

"'SUMMIT: The Achievement of Happiness and Success—The Practical and Spiritual Approach.' You're into self-improvement I see."

"24/7. I always want something more—to do better for myself, my life, in meeting my goals and being happy in the process."

"I'm right there with you." He reached into his bag under the seat in front of him and pulled out a small leather loose-leaf notebook. He unzipped it. "I've got my daily goals, weekly, monthly, quarterly, yearly. And I write what my experiences are in getting to them and making them happen every day."

"Seems like we have a lot in common," Natalie remarked.

"I can only hope. So is there anyone special in your life?" Jeremy inquired.

"Yes, there is," she answered, with a radiant glow in her eyes.

Jeremy took Natalie's hand. "He's a lucky man... And by the way, if you so much as look at another man, Angel, I'll kill you..."

Jeremy's words pierced her soul though the tone of his voice was adoring. Their verbal game was over.

As the plane left the gate, Natalie's heart was racing. She realized that this was the path she had chosen. Natalie stared out the window at the tarmac moving underneath them. She already missed her mother—the only other person for whom Natalie truly cared. Had she made the right decision?

Once airborne and the seat belt sign was turned off, a flight attendant announced that passengers could move freely through the cabin.

Jeremy nodded to Natalie.

She unwrapped her scarf and stuck it in her purse along with her sunglasses.

Jeremy placed his hat under the seat and put his sunglasses in his jacket pocket.

Natalie headed to the lavatory and left the door switched on 'unoccupied.'

Jeremy followed and entered the same lavatory. He locked the door behind them and then lifted Natalie's blouse. Jeremy caressed Natalie's stomach admiring her pregnant glow and nascent maternal beauty. He nibbled at the back of her neck.

"Take me," Natalie said, breathlessly—driven by her hunger for Jeremy.

They made passionate love at 35,000 feet.

"I just want to have you all to myself, Angel," Jeremy said. "No one can know you the way I do. I will always love you, Princess."

"You are my soul mate for eternity," Natalie whispered in his ear.

The plane soared taking them to their lovers' paradise for which they had waited a lifetime. They slipped away to their new life together… without a trace....

Epilogue

When Natalie and Jeremy returned to his house on the beach after their long journey, it seemed as though the last several months had been a dream—a nightmare—that was now over.

"Hey, baby, let me get that," Jeremy said to Natalie taking her suitcase from her.

She stood motionless except for her eyes. She soaked in a panoramic view of where she and Jeremy had made the most tender love, where she had felt the greatest pain—when she realized Jeremy was gone. The two glasses they drank from their last night together were still perched on the center island in the kitchen. The few drops of wine that remained were now eerily dried to the bottom of the crystal goblets. The nascent life within Natalie's stomach was queasy, cramping. Jeremy's home had a haunting silence. Had she made the right decision to return to Cannes—

with Jeremy? She had endured so much to get back to this place where she had felt loved, nurtured, whole.

Jeremy noticed that Natalie was uncomfortable, disturbed. He took her hand and kissed her palm. "It's okay, baby. We're home now. It's all over... Come on," he said, leading Natalie to the door of the deck. Jeremy raised the shade revealing the gentle waves lilting to and fro on the warm beige sand while the sun began to set. He opened the sliding glass door. They stepped outside. Jeremy stood behind Natalie giving her a soothing rub on her growing tummy.

Natalie was calmed by the soft breeze blowing through her hair and the fresh sea air surrounding them. She reached for Jeremy's hand, holding it to her cheek. Jeremy Junior, too, was beginning to feel more calm. The cramping and nausea subsided.

That night, Natalie and Jeremy made magical love again and again—in front of the fireplace, in the outdoor wooden shower, under the billowing sheets of Jeremy's bed. Natalie was swept up in a web of romance she never wanted to end.

"Please don't ever leave me again," Natalie whispered as they lay nestled into one another, spent from their love-making. "Do you think it can always be this way now?"

Jeremy stroked Natalie's head. "It's all up to you, Angel. It's all up to you."

Natalie wasn't sure what he meant by his remark, but she felt nurtured, comforted that Jeremy was near, holding her close. She could feel his heartbeat, hear his breath as he inhaled. Exhaled. While they drifted off to sleep, Natalie was at peace knowing Jeremy's child was growing within her.

The next morning, Natalie and Jeremy met with Santiago at his office.

"I trust you had a good trip in," Enrique said, greeting Jeremy with a handshake. "My dear, Natalie. Motherhood agrees with you. You are as beautiful as ever."

She smiled. "I'm very much looking forward to working together, Enrique. I promise I'll hold up my end of the bargain and keep Jeremy in line during the transition."

Jeremy glared at her.

"I know you won't disappoint me. That's why I hired you. Let me show you around and introduce you both to some of my key, and now, some of your key, people."

"This is my eldest son, Enrique Junior," he said, motioning to the young man seated in his office. "He's the president of the electronics operation you purchased."

"Is this another one of your underhanded tricks?" Jeremy asked with a cold fire burning in his eyes.

"Did I not mention that?" Enrique asked with a snide tone. "If you look carefully at your contract, you requested that my senior management remain in place for a full year. There may have even been an addendum listing them by name. This should come as no surprise if you did your homework."

"Call me EJ," Enrique's son said. "I understand you're going to keep me and my new boss in line," he said to Natalie, extending his hand to shake hers. Their eyes locked. He held her hand softly. "My father did say you were beautiful. I should have believed him..." He dropped his hand. "Jeremy and I are not supposed to interfere with my brother's 'success.' He's heir-to-the-throne of all my father's achievements," he said glancing at his father. "I look forward to working... under you."

Natalie was caught off-guard by EJ's flirtation... and quietly flattered. He was an Adonis—tan, rugged build, broad shoulders, handsome—mouth-watering looks.

Jeremy was infuriated that Enrique's son was making advances toward Natalie—right in front of him. His blood boiled. Was EJ that much of a player to have total disregard for his impending working relationship with Natalie from the beginning? Could he not see she was with child? That she was wearing a wedding ring? This was not what bothered Jeremy. He was irate that Natalie appeared to enjoy the attention from another man.

244

Jeremy kept his professional composure, but Natalie knew he was upset. He hastened Enrique Senior through their 'meet-and-greet' tour. "We had a long day yesterday. What say we pick this up tomorrow, when we're all on local time?"

"Whatever you would like," Enrique said smugly. "It's your baby now."

Once in the car, Jeremy's demeanor seemed to relax somewhat though he was still angry. "Why don't we take the rest of the day and 'play hooky.' Work'll be there tomorrow. I had enough of Enrique one and two for today... Maybe we can catch an amazing sunset. There's an exquisite spot I would love to share with you where the view is spectacular. I can make love to you with the roar of the waves crashing below." Jeremy drove wildly on the narrow, winding roads.

"Can you please slow down? Natalie asked. "You're scaring me. What if someone's coming from the other direction?"

"We're fine. Believe me. Nobody's gonna be up here in the middle of a work day." Suddenly, he slammed on the breaks. "This is it, Angel. We're here. Come on. Let's check it out."

Natalie tried to open her door, but the strong wind held it closed. She pushed as hard as she could. After several seconds of struggling, it opened. A strong gust blew her hair wildly then slammed the door shut.

"It's too breezy up here. Why don't we do this another time?"

Jeremy jogged around to help her out, offering his hand. "Come on."

"I don't want to. It's cold. Let's come back another time."

His nostrils flared.

She could feel his anger wash over her.

"Just take a quick look and then we can go. We drove all the way up here. You at least have to see the view."

"Fine," Natalie said with exasperation. Reluctantly, she appeased him and got out of the car.

Jeremy held her hand as they walked. Suddenly his hand became rigid. His congenial air faded. "What if EJ asked you to do something? Would you defy him?"

"I'm getting back in the car," she snapped.

"I saw you flirt with him. You loved the attention. Admit it. Are you gonna fuck him? I told you, it was all up to you, Angel, and now you've betrayed my love."

Natalie tried to pull her hand from his and turned to race for the car.

Jeremy yanked her back. "You've made me very angry. And now you'll have to pay." He pushed her to the edge of the overlook. "Are you going to betray me again?"

A cold terror filled her body. Natalie struggled to loosen his grip.

"Let me go. You're hurting me," she shouted, wriggling, trying to push him away from her. She could sense the fire in his soul intensifying.

Jeremy thrust her to the ground. He clutched her throat with both hands.

Natalie kneed him in the groin.

He grunted in pain, then pinned her under him. Jeremy reached for a fallen tree branch that was near them. His arm drew back, smashing her skull with it.

"Aaahh!" she groaned, held down by the weight of his body. Blood leaked from her scalp into her left eye. In a flash of a second in her mind, she was under him, fifteen again, being raped by him. "Noooooo!" she screamed from the depth of her soul. "This is not the life I have chosen..." she said trying to catch her breath. "I've been a victim my entire life and I'm not gonna let you do this to me... I didn't give up everything for this. You think you can kill me, you bastard? No fucking way... And I'm not gonna let you kill my child!" Natalie thrashed under him, trying to break free.

Jeremy was enraged, breathing ragged. He stood up, clutching Natalie's hair, lifting her to her feet.

He forced her to the edge of the cliff.

She fought back with every ounce of strength in her body, bracing herself against the ground. Suddenly, she was free from his grasp.

Jeremy lunged for her and they, again, fell to the ground. One hand pressed against her windpipe, the other clutched both her hands.

Natalie was kicking him to get out of his reach. She kept pushing him closer and closer to the edge.

"You will never betray me again!"

She bit his arm, drawing blood.

"You bitch," he screamed, pulling his arm back. Suddenly, he began to lose his balance and started to fall off the edge.

Natalie saw the horror in his eyes sink in as he realized he was tumbling backwards. A sweltering panic filled her body. "Oh, God!" she screamed out.

Jeremy was out of her reach. "Help me," he pleaded, with an outstretched arm as he slipped off the side of the cliff.

"Noooo!" she heard, in a quickly fading scream, as Jeremy fell to his death.

The deafening sound echoed against the cliffs, piercing her brain. She couldn't breathe. Her chest tight. Natalie sobbed uncontrollably trying to catch her breath, her face buried in her hands, blood still dripping from her scalp. Tormented. Without a trace. Jeremy was gone—the only man she ever loved. Natalie and her baby were alive. She fought to have the life she had chosen. No one was going to take that from her.